All C

By

RJ Nolan

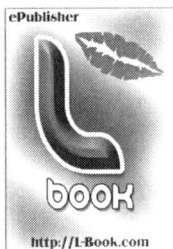

ePublisher

book

http://L-Book.com

All Gone
Lesbian Fiction: Mystery

Print ISBN-13: **978-1-934889-37-1**
eBook ISBN-13: **978-1-934889-09-1**
Audio eBook ISBN-13: **978-0-9800846-0-3**

First Edition
Paperback Format
First Print: July 2009
Published: December 2007

Paperback and electronic books are published by
L-Book ePublisher, LLC
La Quinta, Ca. 92253
Web Site: http://L-Book.com

Executive Editor: Pam

Cover Design by Sheri
graphicartist2020@hotmail.com

Visit Our Web Site at

http://L-Book.com

Acknowledgments

I would like to thank the following people for their help and assistance with this novel. To Pam for her outstanding editing skills and encyclopedic knowledge of all thing related to the use of the English language. To Victoria for her unflagging support and encouragement. To Dr. K. Bader for providing technical and medical information. And last but certainly not least, to Bardeyes and WebWarrior for offering an on-line home to an aspiring author. Your support and encouragement are greatly appreciated.

Dedication

To Thor and Titan, two wonderful Great Danes I have had the privilege of sharing my life with. You lightened my days and brought joy to my life. You are both sorely missed.

All Gone

CHAPTER 1

*D*R. KODY GARRETT smiled down at Blackjack, her fourteen month old Great Dane. "Come on, Jack. It's time to go to work."

The big dog jumped to his feet and began to wag his tail exuberantly. Kody had been working at the North Park Animal Clinic for the last eight months. Since starting to work for Dr. Herbert Donaldson, Jack was only allowed to accompany her to work on the days the senior vet was not present. Before coming to work for Dr. Donaldson, she had worked at another vet clinic. Her previous boss, Dr. Richardson, had loved Blackjack and encouraged her to bring him to work even as a then boisterous young pup. This week was going to be different. For the first time, in the eight months that she had worked for the curmudgeonly vet he was attending a medical conference and left her alone to run the clinic. Although it would make for a long week working alone, she was looking forward to a reprieve of her boss' presence.

Kody shrugged off the troubling thoughts. She loved working at the small clinic and tried her best not to let her boss' gruff manner and poor attitude affect her. It would give her the chance to prove to Dr. Donaldson that she was capable of the responsibility he had entrusted her with. It was going to be a good week, she just knew it.

She could not have been more wrong...

* * *

"Dr. Garrett, we need you in Exam two. Right now."

Kody looked up from the dog she was bandaging. She was immediately concerned by the woman's tone of voice. "What've we got?" she asked. Andrea, a short, slightly overweight brunette was one of her best vet techs.

"Mrs. Daily just walked in with Missy, her Pomeranian. The little dog looks bad. She's very lethargic and her gums are extremely pale," Andrea said.

"Finish up here for me, Mike," she said to the tech who had been assisting her before quickly heading for the exam room.

Kody stepped into the exam room to find a slightly built elderly lady clutching a small dog to her chest.

"Hello, Mrs. Daily. I'm Dr. Garrett. I understand Missy isn't feeling well. Let's take a look at her." She carefully lifted the dog from the woman's arms and placed her gently on the exam table. Kody immediately began to examine the little dog. "So what has been going on with Missy?"

"I don't know. Missy just hasn't been herself for the last few days. She's so tired and hasn't been eating well. I took her outside this morning and she fell trying to climb the steps coming back in. She just wouldn't get up."

"Have you given her anything different, food or medicine?"

"No, just what she always gets."

"Has she been vomiting or had diarrhea?" Kody palpated the dog's abdomen continuing to perform a thorough physical examination as she questioned the owner.

"No, nothing like that. She's just been very tired."

Kody was getting very worried. The dog was unresponsive to stimuli. Its gums were pale with poor capillary refill. Missy's respiratory rate was very high, as was her heart rate while her breathing was very shallow. All the symptoms pointed toward systemic shock, but from what Kody didn't know. She could feel tremors rippling through the little dog's body.

"Is it possible she got into something?" Kody continued her line of questioning trying to narrow the cause of the dog's distress.

"No... She's always with me. What's wrong with her?" Mrs. Daily asked.

Kody had never seen the Pomeranian before. Missy and Mrs. Daily were Dr. Donaldson's clients.

"I'm going to take her in the back and..." The little dog went very still under her hands. She quickly brought her stethoscope down to listen to the dog's heartbeat. She grimaced internally when she didn't find one. *Damn it!* She noticed the dog had released a large puddle of maroon colored stool.

She grabbed the dog and headed for the back room. "Stay here," she said when Mrs. Daily attempted to follow her.

* * *

After trying repeatedly to resuscitate the dog with no success, Kody finally admitted defeat. She reached out and stroked the little dog gently. "It's no good; she's gone," she said to Barbara, the tech who had been helping her.

"Get her cleaned up in case the owner would like to see her," she said before turning to head back to the exam room to give Mrs. Daily the bad news.

Kody walked slowly toward the exam room trying to prepare herself for the ordeal of telling the elderly woman that her dog was dead. This was a part of her job that she had never got used to and knew she never would. She stepped into the exam room and met the woman's eyes.

"I'm so sorry. I did everything I could. She's gone."

Mrs. Daily's eyes filled with tears. "She can't be gone... She can't be. Do something!"

"I did everything I could. I'm very sorry for your loss," Kody said softly.

"I want to see her."

"All right, it will be just a few minutes. I'll come back and get you."

* * *

Mrs. Daily stared at Kody in disbelief, then at her dog lying on the table. "Missy... Missy," she called to the little dog, her voice taking on a slightly hysterical note. "Come on, don't scare Mommy," she said, reaching out and stroking Missy's side. The woman wrapped her arms around her dog and began to sob.

Kody sighed. There was nothing she could do and she had other patients waiting. She took one last look at the little Pom and her broken hearted owner. It just figured, Dr. Donaldson had only been gone a day to his conference and she had already managed to lose one of his patients.

* * *

Kody scrubbed her hands over her face. She had gone over Missy's chart several times trying to spot something she might have missed. There was nothing in her history to explain her sudden demise. Up to this point, she had been a healthy, happy dog. Her most serious medical problem to date had been a severe ear infection due to an embedded foxtail. It just didn't make any sense. Even though the little dog had been eight years old, her annual visit had been only a month ago and Dr. Donaldson had found nothing out of the ordinary on a physical examination. The owner had even consented to running a senior blood panel on Missy for screening purposes. It had come back completely normal.

Kody sighed in frustration; she hated losing a patient. She reached up and rubbed her tight neck muscles. A quiet growl from Blackjack warned her of another's presence just before two warm hands landed on her shoulders and began to massage the tight muscles. Glancing over her shoulder, she looked into the pale green eyes of her vet tech, Barbara. Kody couldn't hold back a groan when the woman hit a particularly tight spot.

The strawberry blond hadn't been working at the clinic for much longer than Kody. She had only been hired a few weeks prior to Kody.

The strong hands kneading the tight muscles of her shoulders felt wonderful and momentarily short-circuited Kody's brain. The ringing of the phone reminded her where she was and how unprofessional her behavior. She liked Barbara and all the staff at the hospital, but strived to maintain a professional relationship with them; anything else would be inappropriate and a big mistake. If they had met under different circumstances, Kody might have been interested in the cute blond; she was just the type she normally went for. But Kody knew in this particular situation that was impossible. She pulled away and reached for the phone.

Barbara reached out and placed her hand on top of Kody's. "I already set up the machine," she whispered near Kody's ear, her hot

- 8 -

breath drawing an involuntary shudder from the woman. As if on cue, Kody heard the automatic voice message click on.

Barbara's hands went back to her shoulders, but Kody pulled away and stood up to face the tech. At five foot nine, she towered over the petite, slenderly built tech.

"Are all the animals settled for the night?" Kody asked with a very neutral look on her face, trying to regain her professional demeanor.

Barbara, over the last few months, had begun to be more familiar than she should with the doctor, saying things that bordered on flirtatious as well as making comments that could be construed as sexual innuendo. It was nothing blatant enough for Kody to call the woman on, but she had felt uncomfortable with the situation. Barbara had tried numerous times to get Kody to go out with her and the other techs after work to socialize. Kody had consistently but politely refused. Tonight had been different. Barbara had never touched her, except for the normal contact of two people working together until tonight. Kody had tried to discourage the woman's interest in her but obviously, she hadn't done enough. She didn't want to alienate anyone she had to work with every day.

Kody tried very hard to keep her personal life personal; she always had. She had grown up in a small town where everyone's personal business was known by everyone else. As she had gotten older, she had grown to resent the small town lifestyle where people knew every where you went, everything you did, and with whom you did it. She and her twin brother, Kyle, were well known. Most days her mother knew what they had been up to even before they got home from school. Kody had realized early that she was not like the other girls, which had added to her sense of alienation. The last thing she wanted to do was mix her personal life with her professional one.

Barbara blinked at Kody's sudden change in demeanor. She had thought she had finally broken through the woman's stand-offish behavior after trying for months to connect with her.

"Yes, everything is locked up and everyone is settled for the night... It's just you and me," she said with a flirtatious smile.

"Good. I'll see you in the morning then," Kody said.

Barbara felt her anger rise at the abrupt brush-off. She took a deep breath and decided to try again. After all, Kody hadn't protested when she massaged her shoulders.

"It's been a hard day, what with losing Missy and all. I know a great little bar not far from here. Let's go for a drink."

Kody now realized that she should have tried harder to nip this in the bud, before she found herself in this situation.

"No thank you," Kody said.

"Come on. It'll be fun," Barbara invited with a warm smile and reached out to stroke Kody's forearm. "It's just two co-workers having a drink together."

Kody knew from Barbara's expression that it was a lot more than that. She tried to put some distance between herself and the tech. Unfortunately, there was not a lot of space to move in her tiny office. Blackjack's blanket took up more than half of the available floor space.

"I'm sorry, no. It's a personal policy of mine. I never socialize with co-workers outside of work."

"It's just a drink," Barbara said. This was not going at all how she planned.

"It has been a long day. I need to get home and feed Blackjack." Kody quickly gathered up her things. She could see how angry the tech was. Calling Blackjack to her side, she quickly made her exit without a backward glance.

Barbara stared after the vet, surprised by her quick exit. "Bitch," she said. *She's just like all the others.* She stared after the dark haired woman and the big dog. She had tried several times to make friends with the dog, but he wanted nothing to do with her. Although she was furious at Kody for turning her down, she couldn't help admiring Kody's curves and shapely ass as she walked away.

CHAPTER 2

"GOOD MORNING, Dr. Garrett," Emily said when Kody stepped into the clinic the next day.

Emily was the most senior staff member aside from Dr. Donaldson. She had started with him shortly after he opened the clinic as a receptionist, and then eventually became the clinic's office manager. Emily enjoyed working with clients and their animals and had continued on with her receptionist duties even after assuming the office manager position. She was in her early fifties and looked after and mothered all the young vet techs. Her figure had spread with middle age, but she was still a good looking woman with wavy brown hair that was lightly streaked with gray and warm, friendly brown eyes.

"Blackjack," she called to the big black dog at Kody's side. "Are you being a good boy?"

The dog wagged his tail and whined, but didn't budge from Kody's side. Kody was thankful that none of the staff shared Dr. Donaldson's poor opinion of giant breed dogs. She still vividly remembered his reaction to his first sight of Blackjack. He had even gone so far as to comment on the fact that he would never understand why someone would want such a huge animal and insinuated the dog was nothing more than a freak novelty. Kody had managed, barely, to keep her temper and made sure never to bring the dog around when Donaldson was working. There were only two Great Danes among their current clientele. She had met the first one within days of starting at the clinic. She smiled fondly at the memory of Kris Rawlings and Willy. Kody had made sure she got to see the other Dane, a beautiful, young, brindle female on her next visit and quickly won over her owners.

Kody opened the short half door and stepped behind the high counter where Emily sat. As soon as she let Blackjack off his leash he headed for Emily and sat down in front of her. The woman laughed, providing him with his morning ear rub and a biscuit.

Blackjack gulped down the biscuit and begged for another, acting like he was starving.

"He did just have breakfast."

"Oh, come on, Doc. He's just a growing boy. Aren't you, Blackjack?" Emily reached out and patted him. The big dog woofed softly and licked Emily's face.

Kody laughed at the pair. Of all the staff at the clinic, Emily was Blackjack's favorite. "Come on, you big mooch, let's go." This was a running battle she had with Emily since the first time she brought Blackjack into the clinic as a then six month old puppy. Left to herself, Emily would stuff him with dog cookies all day.

Blackjack happily trotted over to Kody's side.

"So what do we have on this morning?" Kody asked.

Today was their short day; the clinic was only open until noon on Wednesday. Kody normally didn't work on Wednesdays, but with Dr. Donaldson away at his medical meeting she was covering the clinic every day this week.

Emily looked up at Kody trying not to snicker. "Your favorite patient has an appointment this morning."

Kody narrowed her eyes suspiciously when she spotted the mischievous sparkle in her eyes. She thought about it for several seconds, and then groaned. She couldn't help it.

"Mr. Stevens called and left a message last night. I called him back and he's bringing in Puddles... and he wanted to make sure you would be the one to see her," Emily added, trying to keep a straight face. All the staff was aware of the man's infatuation with Kody.

Mr. Stevens owned an ill tempered, hugely overweight cat. The cat had originally been Dr. Donaldson's patient, but Kody had the misfortune of seeing the cat on her very first day at the clinic. Mr. Stevens had insisted on her seeing Puddles ever since. The cat had hated her on sight, and hissed every time she came near it. The cat's medical problems were exacerbated by the owner's over-feeding and not giving Puddles her prescribed medications. Kody had already had several go-rounds with the cat and had come out of each encounter looking worse for the wear, much to the amusement of her staff.

"What else?" Kody asked.

Emily chuckled sympathetically. "Ms. Philips is bringing in Charlie for a re-check."

Kody smiled. Charlie was the German Shepherd on which she had operated last week. He was a sweet boy who, thankfully, loved her and never gave her trouble. His owner, Ms. Philips, was a vet's dream for a client. She was easy to deal with, very compliant in following instructions and just an all around enjoyable person.

"Okay, I'm going to make some follow-up calls. Let me know when you're ready for me."

Kody glanced into the treatment room and waved to several techs before heading into her office. She was relieved not to have run into Barbara. She got Blackjack settled on his blanket and sat down to do her morning call-backs.

* * *

Kody squared her shoulders and plastered a fake smile on her face before stepping into the exam room.

"Hello, Mr. Stevens."

Mr. Stevens was a short, rotund man in his mid-forties. His dishwater blond hair was coiled up on top of his head in an unsuccessful attempt to cover an ever widening bald spot.

"Perry... Please, call me Perry," he said.

"So what seems to be the problem with Puddles?"

The huge gray cat hissed at her from the safety of her owner's arms.

"Now, now... be nice to the beautiful lady; she's going to make you all better," Mr. Stevens said, stroking the hissing cat's fur gently. He looked up at Kody and gazed into her eyes for several moments. Perry had been attracted to the beautiful, curly haired brunette with the striking gray eyes from the very first time he had seen her. He had asked her out twice before, and she had politely turned him down, stating that she did not date clients. Undaunted he was determined to try again.

Kody shifted uncomfortably and looked away. "What's the problem with Puddles?" she asked again.

"Oh, um..." Mr. Stevens seemed at a loss for words for a moment. Puddles shifting suddenly in his arms seemed to remind him why he was here. "Puddles isn't using her litter box again, and I found what looked like blood mixed with pee on the carpet."

"Have you been giving her the pills I prescribed to acidify her urine?"

Puddles had been treated for a bladder infection and crystals in her urine several months ago.

Mr. Stevens hung his head guiltily. "She doesn't like them and she refuses to eat that special diet. She went the whole morning and wouldn't eat one bite. I got scared and fed her the regular food."

Kody sighed, careful not to let Mr. Stevens hear her. "It's very important that she gets her medication and eats the reduced-calorie food. All this extra weight isn't good for her. Just remember, you're doing it for her own good." They'd had this conversation several times already.

Mr. Stevens refused to meet Kody's eyes.

"I'll need to get a urine sample from Puddles."

"You're going to stick a needle into her bladder again?" Mr. Stevens asked, looking a little green at the thought. "It won't hurt her... right... You promise you won't hurt her?"

Kody preferred not to get a urine sample that way if she could avoid it, but with the uncooperative cat it was a necessity. "I'll sedate her beforehand. She'll be fine. Before I get the urine sample let me check her out, make sure there is nothing else bothering her," she said, holding out her hands to take Puddles.

Mr. Stevens looked hesitant then started to hand Puddles over. The big cat let out a snarl when he tried to place her in Kody's arms. Faster than you would have thought possible for such a large cat, Puddles launched herself at Kody, digging her claws into Kody's lab coat. Before Kody could react, she had thirty pounds of hissing feline attached to her chest. She reached up and grabbed the cat by the scruff of the neck. Puddles snarled in outrage.

"Please don't hurt her!"

"I'm not hurting her," Kody said through gritted teeth as she struggled to control the cat.

Puddles dug her claws in deeper and Kody winced as the sharp claws penetrated her clothing and reached bare skin.

"Wait here. I'll just take her into the back and examine her there," Kody said as calmly as she could.

She quickly hurried out the door with the snarling, hissing feline digging in for all she was worth.

"Help!" Kody called as soon as she stepped into the treatment room.

Mike looked up at his boss and stared at her in disbelief then started to laugh. The stocky, fair haired, ex-marine with his high and tight hair cut looked like he belonged on a Marine Corps recruiting poster. He had come to the clinic as a vet tech after a four-year stint in the Marines.

Kody glared at Mike when he started laughing. "Now!"

Lisa stepped into the room as Mike promptly donned a pair of heavy gloves that reached up to his elbows. Quickly realizing the predicament Dr. Garrett had gotten herself into, she hurried over to help. With Lisa's help, Mike managed to pry the hissing animal off Kody.

"Let's get her sedated," Kody said as soon as she was free. She glanced down at her lab coat and muttered a curse. There was a distinct yellow spot on the front of her lab coat. The smell of urine was unmistakable. Not only had Puddles clawed her, she had urinated on her as well.

She looked up and scowled at the techs when she heard several snickers. Mike and Lisa quickly turned away before Kody could see their grins. Kody worked quickly once the sedative kicked in. She thoroughly examined the cat and got a fresh urine sample.

After donning a fresh lab coat, she carried the now calm cat back to its owner to explain just what needed to be done for the animal, although she didn't have a lot of hope that the owner would comply with her instructions.

* * *

Kody looked up when the door to the exam room opened. She was in the midst of checking Charlie's incision site.

"Dr. Garrett, excuse me for interrupting, but we need you in the back," Lisa said.

Despite the tech's calm manner, Kody could see the urgency in her hazel eyes. Lisa was the youngest of the technicians at twenty one. The lanky redhead was turning into a solid, reliable vet tech. Kody had spoken with the techs previously about unnecessarily alarming clients. She quickly excused herself to Ms. Philips and followed the tech out.

"What've we got?" she asked, hurrying after the tech toward the treatment room.

"The Palmers just brought in Buddy. He's totally unresponsive."

"Damn it," Kody said.

Buddy was a seven year old mixed breed dog. He had presented two months ago with his owner's, who complained that he was lethargic, not eating and was losing his hair along both sides of his body. Blood work had turned up that he had hypothyroidism. With supplementation, he had been steadily improving. On his last visit, two weeks ago, he had appeared a happy, energetic little dog. Now Kody wondered if she had missed something. She found Barbara bent over the dog with a stethoscope pressed to his chest.

Barbara looked up at Kody and shook her head.

Kody's shoulders slumped. She couldn't believe it; Buddy was the second patient to die in two days. First Missy, yesterday, and now Buddy, today. Animals died frequently. It was a sad fact due to their much shorter life spans, but not like this. These were two apparently healthy dogs.

"Did you ever get a heartbeat?" Kody asked, stepping up next to the tech, hoping she would be able to resuscitate the dog.

"No. He was already gone when I checked him," Barbara said.

Kody pressed her stethoscope to the dog's chest confirming there was no heart beat. Sighing heavily, she looked over the little dog. She frowned when she spotted a hematoma on one ear. Looking a bit closer, she noticed a bruise on his belly where his hair was white and very thin. Kody wondered what, if anything, the bruising had to do with Buddy's sudden demise.

Kody looked up at Barbara; she blinked wondering at the expression she had seen before the woman schooled her features into a more neutral appearance. Kody brushed it off, figuring the woman was still angry about last night and turned her concern to the Palmer's.

"Are the Palmers in a room?"

"No. They're waiting out front," Lisa said. She had remained while Kody examined the dog.

Kody sighed. "Okay, put them in a room and I'll be there as soon as I finish up with Charlie."

* * *

Kody forced a smile onto her face and stepped back into the exam room where Charlie and Ms. Philips were waiting.

"I'm sorry to keep you waiting."

Ms. Philips looked at Kody closely and reached out to lay a gentle hand on her arm. "Is everything all right?"

Kody started in surprise and stared for a second at the pretty red-head. She obviously needed to work on hiding her feelings better, but Buddy's death had really upset her. "Um... yes. Charlie is fine. His incision looks great," she said intentionally appearing to misunderstand Ms. Philips.

Ms. Philips raised her eyebrow at Kody but chose not to comment further. "That's great to hear," she said with a warm smile.

Kody finished up with Ms. Philips and Charlie, then headed into exam one to give Buddy's owners the bad news.

* * *

Kody looked over when Blackjack whined. The big dog was stretched out on the floor behind her chair. Glancing at the clock, she was surprised to see how late it was. It was well past his dinner time.

She had spoken to the Palmers at length. They had insisted that Buddy had been perfectly fine until a week ago. He had become lethargic again and they had thought that he might need his medication adjusted. They had called the clinic the day before yesterday and had been scheduled to bring Buddy in tomorrow. The Palmers had arrived home from work and found Buddy lying on the kitchen floor in a large pool of strangely colored feces.

As soon as she had gotten home, Kody had sat down in her study and began going over her books and searching the internet for something that would explain what happened to Buddy and now, she realized, possibly Missy as well.

Kody had come up with several possible causes, but one stood out from the rest. She sent up a silent prayer that in this case, she was wrong. She would have to contact both owners first thing tomorrow.

CHAPTER 3

KODY STRETCHED her tight back muscles and sighed. She was glad the day was almost over. Yesterday, for the first time ever, she had dreaded coming into work. After losing two patients in two days, she had cringed every time she was called into a room with an emergency. They had all turned out well, for which she was very grateful. She didn't think she could have handled losing another animal so soon.

She had talked to both Mrs. Daily and Mrs. Palmer, but neither had been able to give her any further insight into their animals' demise.

Today, Kody had come into the clinic in a better frame of mind. It had been busy all day; she had not even had time for lunch. All she needed to do now was finish one last check of the in-house patients, and then she and Blackjack could head home.

Kody knelt down to open the crate of a little Jack Russell Terrier she had operated on a week ago. Dancer had jumped down from his owner's tall, four poster bed and subluxated his patella. He had required surgery to stabilize his knee.

"Hey, little guy. How are you feeling? Ready to go home tomorrow?"

The little dog jumped up and his whole rear end began to wag as he barked excitedly. The Smiths had several young children and had asked if Dancer could stay at the clinic for the first week after his surgery. Mrs. Smith was worried the energetic little dog would do himself injury. He loved the children and she knew it was going to be difficult to keep him from over doing it once he got home. He lived to play with their three young children and they loved him just as much.

Dancer had been improving every day. Kody lifted the dog out of the crate to check his knee brace. It was like trying to examine a whirling dervish. The dog was in perpetual motion, squirming trying to get down. Kody was distracted for a second by the dog in the next crate and that was all Dancer needed. He twisted himself out of Kody's hands and took off. Even with the brace on his rear leg, the little dog was fast.

"Shit!" Kody took off after the runaway dog. She caught sight of him just as he rounded the corner and ducked into the doorway to one of the exam rooms. Kody swore colorfully when she realized the door leading to the lobby on the other side of the exam room was open. She sprinted toward the little dog and bent over at the waist as she reached out to grab him just as he exited the exam room. Kody's attention was totally focused on Dancer.

"Come here, Dancer!"

Dancer easily ducked around a pair of legs that suddenly appeared in his path – Kody was not as agile as the little dog. Too late, she realized, someone was standing directly outside the exam room door. She tried to stop, but her feet slid on the slippery linoleum floor. She plowed into the person like a linebacker making a tackle. They both went down – hard.

Kody gasped and her breath left in a whoosh as she landed on top of a very firm body. She was stunned by the force of the fall. Shaking her head to clear the daze, she lifted herself up and looked into the face of the woman she had flattened. Her breath caught and she stared into the deepest green eyes she had ever seen. It was like looking into a living emerald. Even more striking than their vivid color was the gold starburst that circled the dark irises.

Kody was brought back to her senses by the woman's deep, husky voice. "Comfy?" The fine lines around the woman's eyes crinkled when a smirk appeared on her face.

Kody blushed furiously, realizing how intimately they were pressed together. "I'm so sorry... I am... I..."

Not only was she lying stretched out full length on top of the woman, but she also had no idea how long she had been staring mesmerized into her eyes.

The woman laughed. "Apology accepted. Now, maybe you could let me up?"

Kody cringed at the laughter the woman's remark caused and realized they had an audience. In her hurry to get off the woman, Kody's knee slipped and she kneed her directly between the legs.

She flinched at the woman's pained grunt. Kody scrambled to her feet and offered the woman a hand to help her off the floor, apologizing profusely the whole time.

BJ stared at the admittedly beautiful brunette with her short, dark curly hair and striking gray eyes. Noticing the lab coat for the first time, she realized this must be the vet who had called the office. She gazed at the brunette's hand suspiciously, wondering if she dared take it. In a matter of minutes, the woman had slammed her to the floor, and then kneed her.

"It's okay... no problem," BJ said as the vet continued to apologize.

BJ reached out cautiously and accepted the woman's hand her eyes widening in surprise when her fingers tingled at the vet's touch. When she regained her feet, BJ bent over slightly with her hands placed on her thighs, fighting the instinct to cup her painfully throbbing sex. The woman had nailed her, but good.

Kody was at a total loss for words, confused by her body's reaction to the simple touch of the other woman's hand. When the woman stood to her full height, Kody got her first good look at her. She was tall, easily matching Kody's five foot nine stature. But she was stockier built and worked out, if the toned biceps and forearms showing below the sleeve of her shirt were any indication. Her dark hair was clipper cut, extremely short on the sides and back in a very masculine style, then a bit longer and spiked on top. Strangely, the haircut didn't seem the least bit masculine on the woman; she was handsome without appearing manly.

Emily looked at her boss worriedly. She hadn't said a word after the officer had waved off her repeated apologies and just stood mutely staring at the woman.

"Dr. Garrett, this is Officer BJ Braden and her partner, Officer Neil Martin," Emily said.

Kody flushed and shook herself out of her stupor, realizing that she had been staring again. She had been so shaken up by everything that she hadn't even registered that the woman was wearing a uniform. Noticing the man standing nearby in a matching uniform for the first time, she looked over at Officer Braden's partner. He was incredibly handsome with sun-bleached blond hair and dark vivid blue eyes. Kody estimated he must be at least six foot five. He looked like he belonged on a movie set somewhere instead of her lobby.

Neil grinned at the vet. "Did you by chance lose this?" he asked, holding a squirming Dancer in one of his big hands.

As seemed her perpetual state this evening, Kody's face once again flushed with color. "Thanks," she said as she took the little dog from the officer. "You're in big trouble, little man," she muttered drawing a laugh from the two officers.

Turning back to business, she looked at the two visitors questioningly, wondering why animal control officers were in her lobby. "What can I do for you, Officers?"

"We got a report yesterday that you had called concerning two dogs that died. Sorry, we couldn't get here sooner," BJ said.

Yesterday had been so hectic that Kody had totally forgotten about the call she had put in to animal control.

Kody smiled at the two officers. "Thanks for coming down. Just let me put this little trouble maker back in his crate, and I'll be right with you." She turned toward the receptionist. "Emily, could you take the two officers into Dr. Donaldson's office and I will be right in." Kody knew there wasn't room for the three of them to meet in her small office.

* * *

Kody had taken a few minutes, after putting Dancer away, to regain her composure. She didn't know what had come over her after she ended up on top of the decidedly androgynous but extremely good looking officer. It wasn't like her to peruse someone like that. Not to mention the fact that the officer wasn't the type of woman she was usually attracted to. She stepped into Dr. Donaldson's large office and found both officers already seated in front of his desk. They rose as she entered.

Kody smiled. "Please have a seat." She took a seat behind the desk. "Officer Braden, I want to apologize again for what happened. I'm really sorry, and I hope you're okay."

"It's BJ, and apology accepted."

Kody nodded her thanks and looked at the two officers expectantly.

Neil flipped open his notebook and quickly turned to business. "Now, Dr. Garrett, what has you concerned about the two deaths you reported?"

Kody quickly explained what had happened to the two dogs.

"So I'm assuming you don't think the deaths were from natural causes?" Neil asked.

"I researched the possible causes of the symptoms both dogs presented that could explain their respective demises. There are a number of conditions that could cause the same symptoms. But after speaking extensively to each owner and reviewing each dog's medical history, I feel there is a strong possibility that these two dogs were poisoned. I checked their patient records and they live within three blocks of each other. I wasn't able to convince either owner to allow me to perform a necropsy and both dogs have been sent for cremation. At this point, I have nothing but my suspicions, but I wanted to inform animal control of a potential problem. Is there anything you can do?" she asked, looking at the officers beseechingly.

"Think it may be a case of accidental poisoning?" BJ asked.

"That, I don't know. I certainly hope so, but to have two dogs come in only a day apart, with the same symptoms, worries me."

"If you'll give us the name and addresses of the owners we'll look into it," Neil said.

Kody hesitated. "I really don't want to upset the owners with what are, at this point, unfounded suspicions. I spoke to both owners yesterday and neither had anything to add to what had happened and both were still extremely distraught."

BJ nodded. "We understand that. The loss of a beloved pet at the best of times is devastating without adding the possibility of the animal having been poisoned, however unintentionally. We'll simply tell the owners we are conducting an investigation on pet health in their neighborhood. We won't inform them that it has anything to do with their dogs until we have more information. It may be something as simple as someone in the neighborhood who is having a rodent problem and used poison, not realizing the impact it can have on other animals."

"Great. I'll have Emily —"

Kody was cut off when the office door opened suddenly. One look at her tech's face and she was on her feet before Andrea could say a word.

"Excuse me," she said as she hurried out of the room.

* * *

"What have we got?"

"Mrs. Quinn just brought in Blackie, her lab. He's bleeding from his nose; his gums are pale; respiratory rate is high. His breathing is very labored, pulse is weak and thready."

No! Not again, Kody thought as she raced to the dog's side. Blackie was a two year old Labrador Retriever. Kody had seen him not two months ago for his annual physical. He was a healthy, active young dog.

She quickly examined the panting black lab. He had large hematomas on both ears and was bleeding from his nose. His lungs sounded congested and he was struggling for every breath.

"Draw blood on him. I want a routine panel as wells as a PT PTT and get a chest x-ray STAT!" Kody ordered as she inserted an IV into the dog's leg and got some fluid running. She wanted an open line in case she needed to resuscitate him. She placed an oxygen mask over his muzzle, trying to give the struggling animal some air.

The techs quickly went into action, carrying out Kody's instructions. Kody headed to the front lobby to talk to the owners. She found them alone in the waiting room.

Mrs. Quinn was bent over at the waist, her hands covering her face, sobbing uncontrollably. Her husband sat next to her patting her shoulder consolingly. He stood and stuck out his hand to Kody when he spotted her.

"Dr. Garrett."

Time was of the essence. She didn't waste any on pleasantries. "Tell me what happened to Blackie," Kody said.

"We're not sure what happened. He's been acting kind of funny for the last few days, really tired, not eating well, and not wanting to play with the kids. And that's his favorite thing, isn't it honey?" he asked his wife. She nodded and began to cry harder. "It's okay, honey. He's going to be okay... isn't he?" he asked, his eyes begging Kody for reassurance.

Kody's shoulders slumped a bit but she forced a neutral expression on her face. This was sounding ominously familiar. "We are still running tests. It's too soon to say what's wrong," Kody said. "What happened tonight? When he started bleeding?"

"I wasn't there. My wife called me at work. Honey, you need to tell the doctor what happened, so she can help Blackie."

Mrs. Quinn visibly fought to pull herself together. She looked up at Kody with anguished eyes. "Please don't let him die."

"I'll do every thing I can," Kody said. "Anything that you can tell me would help."

"Blackie's been coughing a little bit the past two days. It didn't seem like it was anything serious. I thought maybe he just had a bit of a cold and that was why he wasn't eating. I was in the kitchen making dinner when one of the kids started screaming. I ran into the family room. Blackie was coughing really hard, like he had something stuck in his throat. He seemed to be having trouble breathing, and then all the sudden, blood started to pour from his nose." Mrs. Quinn broke down and began to sob. "I should have brought him in sooner."

"Has he had any diarrhea or vomiting?" Mrs. Quinn shook her head. "Is it possible he got into something?" Kody continued to question the distraught woman. She needed as much information as she could get.

"Our yard borders the junior high school. Those damn kids are forever throwing stuff in our yard at Blackie when he barks at them, so it's possible," Mr. Quinn said. "I've spoken to the principal over there several times and he's never done anything about those little delinquents."

Mrs. Quinn pattered her husband's arm trying to calm him. "All that matters now is Blackie," she said.

"All right, if there is anything else you can think of let the receptionist know. I need to get back to Blackie. I'll come back out as soon as I know anything.

The couple nodded gratefully. Kody turned and quickly headed for the treatment room.

* * *

Kody went directly to the view box when she saw Blackie's x-ray had been hung. She immediately noticed an opacity in Blackie's lung on the film. Normally, she would assume pneumonia but with his other symptoms, she felt it was more than likely that it was blood. If what she suspected was wrong with Blackie was the case, she didn't have time to wait for the blood test to come back from the lab that would confirm her suspicion. She needed to act now.

"Andrea, get me a vial of Vitamin K, then see if any of our donor dogs are available just in case we need to give him a transfusion."

Andrea's eyes widened. She quickly realized what Dr. Garrett suspected. She hurried off to get what the doctor needed for Blackie.

Kody drew up an injection of Vitamin K, which was the antidote for rat poisoning. The chemical used to poison rodents interfered with the target animal's blood clotting factors, causing it to eventually bleed to death. Unfortunately, it had the same effect on any other animal that had the misfortune to ingest it. She stroked the distressed dog, then quickly injected him with the Vitamin K. Knowing she had done all she could for the moment, she headed out to the lobby to once again face the Quinns.

* * *

Kody stopped in the hall when she heard her name called. She turned to find the two animal control officers walking toward her. She had forgotten all about them.

"What's going on?" BJ asked. She had known something was wrong when Dr. Garrett rushed out of the office.

Kody sighed in frustration. "I think we've just had another poisoning, if that's what is going on. I just don't know for sure." She quickly explained to the two officers what had happened. "I'm going out to talk to the family now."

"Is the dog still alive?" Neil asked.

"Thankfully, yes. I've started him on Vitamin K. If it is rat poisoning, as I suspect, then he should show some improvement by morning. I had a PT PTT drawn on him. It won't be back from the lab until first thing tomorrow. We don't have the facilities to perform that type of test here. That will tell us for sure if his clotting factors are elevated as rat poison would do. I'll draw blood again tomorrow and have the test repeated. We should see some change in the clotting factors if the Vitamin K is working. While it's not conclusive proof that he was poisoned, unless I find something else that points to another cause, it's the closest we're going to get. As you know, there is no specific test for rat poison; it's diagnosed by process of elimination."

"All right, we'll check back with you on Monday to see what the lab results are," Neil said.

Kody nodded. She watched as the two walked away, her eyes unconsciously lingering on the muscled form of Officer Braden. When they disappeared from sight, she headed toward the lobby and the waiting Quinns.

* * *

Kody scrubbed her hands over her face. The meeting with the Quinns had not gone well. When Kody had explained her suspicions, Mr. Quinn had just about blown a gasket. He vowed to find the 'little bastards' who had done this and hang them out to dry. It had taken his wife quite some time to calm him down. Kody had quickly reiterated that she had no proof at this point, but was treating Blackie just in case.

She looked down at the black head resting comfortably on her thigh. "Hang in there, Blackie," she said as she stroked the dog's head. Her first real smile in hours graced her face when his tail thumped on the floor. He seemed to be holding his own and breathing more easily.

She looked up when she heard someone enter the treatment area. Kody smiled up at Tom. The short, slimly built young man with shaggy black hair and round wire-rimmed glasses covering big brown eyes was one of her techs. He didn't work full time, but whenever they had a patient who needed 'round-the-clock care he would come in and spend the night in the clinic.

"Hey, Tom. How are you tonight?"

"I'm good, Dr. Garrett. How is this big guy doing?" Andrea had filled him in on what was happening when she called to request he work tonight.

"Much better than earlier, that's for sure."

She quickly gave the tech an update on the dog's condition. It was late and she had sent the other techs home over an hour ago. Andrea had volunteered to wait for Tom to arrive, but Kody had sent her on her way, wanting to stay with the dog for a bit longer.

"Thanks for coming in, Tom. I appreciate it."

"No problem. Where's your big guy?"

"Last time I looked he was snoring away in my office. In my next life, I want to come back as a dog," Kody said.

Tom laughed. "Go home and get some rest, Doctor G. I'll take good care of this guy. Don't you worry."

"I won't. I know he's in good hands. Have a good night, Tom, and call me immediately if there is any change. We do have one of our donor dogs and their owner standing by if needed."

Tom nodded, his attention already focused on Blackie.

Kody wearily made her way to her office. She woke up the big lump on the floor and headed for her truck.

CHAPTER 4

"*E*XCUSE ME, Dr. Garrett."

Kody looked up from the chart she was working on and scowled. "What is it, Barbara?"

Blackjack wasn't as restrained and growled at the tech from his bed, earning a stern look and reprimand from his owner.

Kody had been less than happy to find out Barbara was the tech who would be closing up the clinic today. She normally didn't work on Saturdays and Kody had been surprised to see her. The woman had been prissy all morning, and Kody was fed up with her. Thankfully, they only worked a half day on Saturday and the patient load had been unusually light today. Mike had left a half an hour ago, leaving the two of them to finish up and shut down the clinic. Kody just wished Tom would hurry up and get here so she wouldn't have to spend time alone with the disgruntled tech.

"There's a woman out front asking to see you. I told her she had to make an appointment, but she insists on speaking to you."

"Did she say what it was about?"

Barbara shrugged dismissively. "Just something about a dog."

What the hell kind of answer was that? Kody didn't know what Barbara thought she was pulling, but much more of this and Kody was going to have to talk to Dr. Donaldson when he got back, and damn the consequences. Regrettably, she didn't have the authority to fire a tech or she would seriously consider it, if Barbara's attitude didn't improve.

Kody rose from her chair. "Thank you, I'll take care of it."

Barbara stood in the doorway and stared at Kody, making no attempt to move.

"Excuse me," Kody said.

Barbara moved aside slightly but not enough to allow Kody to pass without brushing against her.

Kody had had enough. "Don't you have work to do?" she said. She glared down at the tech, refusing to be forced to brush against her in passing.

Barbara's face flushed angrily and she spun on her heels and headed back toward the front desk.

Kody took a moment to regain her temper, and then followed the tech to the front of the clinic. She smiled when she spotted the woman on the other side of the counter. She wasn't in uniform today, but dressed instead in a skin-hugging black tee shirt and jeans that displayed her extremely well toned physique. Kody felt a sudden flush when she remembered being tightly pressed against that hard body. She hadn't expected to see the officer until Monday.

Forcing herself into a more professional mode, Kody greeted the woman. "Hello, Officer Braden. You on-call today?"

BJ smiled at Kody. After they left last night, Neil had a great time teasing her about the vet knocking her down. BJ grinned wolfishly at the memory of the doctor's lush body on top of hers. She couldn't stand the rail-thin women who seemed to be all the rage these days. The beautiful vet was not overweight by any stretch of the imagination, but BJ was willing to bet she had some nice womanly curves under that white lab coat. Shaking herself out of her lustful thoughts, she turned her attention to business.

"Hey, Dr. Garrett. No. I just wanted to stop by and see how the dog from last night was doing. Blackie... right?"

"Umm... yeah, Blackie, that's right," Kody said, momentarily distracted by the fleeting expression that had covered BJ's face. "Come on back and I'll introduce you to him."

BJ stepped over to the half gate that separated her from the vet. She glared at the tech who had given her such a hard time when she asked to see the doctor.

* * *

BJ sat on the floor and stroked the head of the big black lab. He had wagged his tail weakly when Kody opened the door to his crate. BJ hadn't been able to resist the silent plea in his big brown eyes.

"With his clotting times so elevated, I'm more convinced than ever that Blackie ingested rat poison," Kody said, flipping through the pages of the dog's chart. "The owners also told me that they have been having problems with kids from the school next door to them. It seems some of the kids have been throwing things over their fence at the dog."

BJ shook her head in disgust. "If you'll give me the owner's name and address, Neil and I will go by there on Monday and see if they'll allow us to do a search of the yard."

"That's the other thing I wanted to tell you. I checked the records. The Quinns, Blackie's owners, live on the same street as the Palmers, who owned Buddy – one of the other dogs I told you about last night."

"Son of a bitch," BJ said. She had been an animal control officer long enough to have developed some pretty good instincts, and right now they were screaming that something was definitely not right here.

"Yeah, that's pretty much what I said when I saw the Quinns' address."

BJ blushed when she realized Kody had heard her curse. She stood up and offered the vet her hand. Kody had been sitting down on the other side of Blackie's crate as she went over his chart with her.

Kody smiled and took the offered hand. She almost pulled away when her fingers started to tingle at the first touch of BJ's skin. From the look on BJ's face, it was obvious she had felt it too.

"So, umm...you'll let me know what you find at the Quinns?" Kody asked, trying to stay professional and ignore the strange tingling in her fingers.

BJ was still trying to figure out why she got an unaccustomed, but not unpleasant sensation every time the vet touched her. She shook her head, realizing the doctor had spoken to her.

"What? Oh yeah. We'll stop by and let you know what, if anything, we find out. This will also give us a good excuse to talk to the Palmers, since they live on the same street."

Kody held out a piece of paper with the Quinn's name and address on it, as well as the two other dog owners. With the excitement of Blackie's arrival the officers had left without the owner information of the other dogs. "Thank you, Officer Braden. I appreciate you letting me know anything you find out. I just hope we can keep this from happening to any other dogs."

"I told you, it's BJ. And I promise you, Neil and I will do our best to find out who's doing this," BJ said with a warm smile.

Kody smiled brightly. She liked this woman. Her caring and compassion for the animals she looked out for was evident in her voice. She knew for a fact that animal control officers didn't work on the weekend, unless on-call. So the fact that BJ had taken the time, on her day off to check on Blackie showed just how dedicated she was.

"Thanks, BJ."

The two women said their good-byes. BJ headed out of the clinic, sending one last glare at the irritating tech on her way out. Kody headed back into her office to finish up her paperwork.

CHAPTER 5

NEIL TOOK A deep sniff of the cup of coffee that appeared in front of him from over his shoulder. "You're a goddess," he said as he took the cup. He didn't even bother to look back to see who was holding the cup. BJ regularly stopped and bought coffee for them on her way to work.

BJ snorted. "Sure... sure, you'd say that to any woman who brought you a red-eye." She took her own cup of coffee out of the holder and sat down opposite Neil at their shared partner's desk.

She laughed at the orgasmic look on Neil's face as he took his first gulp. He loved his coffee and dark Kenya roast with a double shot of espresso was his favorite.

Now, if I could just get a woman to look at me like that, BJ thought wishfully.

BJ couldn't even remember exactly when the last time she was out on a date. It wasn't for lack of interest. The long hours she put in, plus the animals she frequently fostered when she wasn't working, didn't leave a lot of free time. She had even given up her gym membership and created a workout room at home so she had more time to devote to the abused animals she cared for. All in all, it didn't leave a lot of time or opportunity to meet a woman, much less develop a relationship with one. BJ had indulged in a number of one night stands in her younger days, but in recent years just wasn't interested in that type of mindless sex. Maybe she was just one of those people who were destined to be alone. Now, if she could find someone that shared her passion for the animals she looked out for every day – like the beautiful vet she had met last week.

"Earth to BJ."

BJ shook her head realizing Neil must have called her several times. "Sorry, what were you saying?" She pushed away the depressing thoughts and turned her mind back to work.

"Where were you? You looked a million miles away. Is everything all right?"

BJ brushed his concern aside. "I'm fine. A baby kitten kept me up last night," she lied. Although she had taken two young kittens home, after their midnight feeding, they had slept through the night.

Neil nodded understandingly. It wasn't uncommon for BJ to take home several babies that required around-the-clock care over the weekend.

Neil shook his head a bit sadly. "You, my friend, need to get a life."

He worried that BJ didn't seem to have a life outside of work. She frequently stayed long after working hours, chasing some case or paperwork. Although they had been colleagues for almost five years, he had never heard her even mention going out somewhere on the weekend or after work, much less actually dating someone. He was aware of the fact that BJ was a lesbian; it wasn't as if she was trying to hide her personal life. She didn't have one. The only person she ever mentioned, and even that was rarely, was her sister. He cared about the animals as well, but was concerned about BJ. Her whole life it seemed was dedicated to the welfare of the animals they saw abused on a daily basis.

"Hell, forget the life. You just need to get out of the house occasionally and have some fun!" Neil said.

BJ scowled at Neil, refusing to be baited. She knew what kind of life Neil led. "There are more important things in life than getting laid as often as you can with as many different women as you can. That's not a life."

"Don't knock it 'til you've tried it. Sure as hell beats going home and snuggling up to a warm puppy," Neil said.

BJ glared at Neil; they had had this argument before. They worked well together, and she loved him like a brother, but she absolutely despised the way he used women. Granted, the women were more than willing, and more frequently than not were the ones that threw themselves at Neil, but she still hated it.

"Christ, just forget it. I'm sorry I even mentioned it." Neil scowled in frustration. "What have we got on today?" he asked, referring to their day's assignments.

BJ shrugged off the sting of Neil's words and tried to concentrate on business. "We've got several follow-up calls and quite a few new ones. I want to follow up on that shooting case. I've just got a gut feeling Mrs. Brunner saw something."

Mrs. Brunner was the neighbor across the street from the Chadwick's. Their dog, Brutus had been shot with some type of pellet gun the previous week. When they originally questioned everyone in the neighborhood, she had denied seeing anything.

Neil nodded in acknowledgement as he made notations in his notebook. "Okay, let's hit all the follow-ups first, then we'll take as many of the new calls as we can."

"All right. We also need to contact the owners of the dogs Dr. Garrett told us about."

"Right, I forgot about that. We'll swing by the clinic and see if the dog survived the weekend and get the addresses we need."

"He's doing fine and I've got the owner's information," BJ said and turned to pick up her gear.

"Oh, did the vet already call in?"

BJ looked away, knowing Neil was going to give her a hard time. "No. I stopped by the clinic on Saturday and checked on him."

"Damn it, BJ!"

"Just drop it! I don't want to hear it, Neil. What I do with my time off is my business."

"That's just the point... it's called time off from work. You're supposed to do something besides work. But what do you do? You go check on some dog. You need to get away from all this, if only for a little while. I'm worried about you, BJ; you'll burn yourself out."

BJ sighed. She knew Neil was concerned about her, but it was her life and she was happy with it. *That's right, you just keep telling yourself that.* BJ rubbed her tight neck muscles and forced herself to focus on what was important – the animals.

"Let's go. We've got a lot of cases to cover," BJ said before walking out of the office.

Neil blew out a breath in frustration and followed his partner out to their truck.

CHAPTER 6

"**Y**OU DID **WHAT**! What the hell were you thinking? No, wait, obviously you weren't."

Kody winced, sure that the whole clinic had heard Dr. Donaldson even through the closed office door. He had returned from his medical conference and Kody had been bringing him up to date about what had transpired at the clinic in his absence. She had just informed him that she had called in Animal Control about the dogs that had died. Kody had a feeling he would not be happy about her calling in the agency, but had not expected quite this response.

Kody sighed. By now you think she would have learned and not been the least bit surprised. Most of what Dr. Donaldson chastised her about her work and interaction with the clients was its impact on 'his' clinic's image. "How would this look to the client?" he frequently asked. To him his image and the reputation of the clinic was everything. It didn't matter if it was right or wrong, just how it would affect his perceived image.

"There were two dogs in two days that died, both presented with similar symptoms. Neither had any major medical problems," Kody said, trying to explain her reasons for calling in the animal control officers. "The third dog survived after I treated him for rat poisoning. Two of the clients live on the same street and the third only three blocks away."

Dr. Donaldson's face turned even redder and the veins in his forehead started to pulse. Not a particularly handsome man to start with, his anger turned his normally splotchy complexion even more mottled. "And I suppose you gave these animal control people our clients' private information–like their names and addresses?"

Dr. Donaldson slapped the palm of his hand against his desk in anger when Kody nodded, his temper rising with every word. "Do you know what kind of panic you could cause with this? What do you think our clients are going to think when they see animal control officers in our clinic? Or God forbid the clients of the effected dogs sue us, because their dogs died under YOUR care! This is totally irresponsible on your part, Dr. Garrett. I realize now I never should've left you alone in the clinic; obviously you're too inexperienced to handle it."

He swept his hand across his desk, scattering the patient files they had been reviewing.

"But, we're required to report –" Kody said.

"Dogs die every day and we don't always know why. Get used to it. It's our job to comfort and console our clients, not upset them with ridiculous and totally unfounded speculation. In the future, do not contact Animal Control or any other animal welfare agency without my express permission. I only hope I've gotten back soon enough to nip this in the bud. You are not to mention this to anyone again. Is that perfectly clear?"

Kody's hands were clenched in her lap during Dr. Donaldson's rant. She wondered if he was going to stroke out on the spot. His face was purple and the veins in his neck distended from shouting. She knew that she had done the right thing in informing animal control, but she worked for him and had no choice but to follow his dictates, or quit.

"Yes, sir."

"Good. There are clients waiting to be seen. Get back to work," he said.

* * *

As she made her way into the treatment area, Kody couldn't help comparing Dr. Donaldson to her last boss, Dr. Dale Richardson. After completing her internship at a large multi-specialty veterinary hospital she had decided that type of medicine wasn't for her. She had sought out and accepted a position with Dr. Richardson at his small animal hospital. She had learned so much from him in the two years he had been her mentor. He had died suddenly of a massive heart attack. She still mourned his passing. He and his wife had treated her more like a daughter than an employee.

That was the main reason she had chosen to work with Dr. Donaldson, instead of joining a large practice. She had enjoyed working one on one with Dale and hoped to have that same type of learning experience with Dr. Donaldson. She also enjoyed the closer relationship possible only with clients and their animals in a smaller practice. As it turned out, nothing could have been further from reality. Working with Dr. Donaldson was nothing like working with Dale. During her initial interview he had made a big deal about the fact that he wanted to hire a young vet, so that he could mentor them and groom them so they could some day take over his practice. She had fallen for it hook, line and sinker. Kody later found out that she was just one of a string of young vets the doctor had hired and fired. What he claimed he was looking for when he hired her and what his real agenda was were two very different things.

CHAPTER 7

$\mathcal{B}$J SMILED IN satisfaction as they walked toward their truck. They had contacted Mrs. Brunner again and this time, she had admitted to seeing her neighbor's son with a rifle. They had questioned the young man and his parents. After repeated denials the youth had finally confessed to shooting the dog. He had broken down in tears, claiming he had taken his pellet rifle out just for a little target practice and had accidentally shot the next door neighbor's dog. His father had been furious and promised that the boy would be punished as well as having to work to pay for the injured dog's vet bills. Luckily, the dog had survived and was recovering well after surgery to remove the pellet from his shoulder.

Because the boy was twelve years old and, therefore, a minor, he would not be charged with animal cruelty, but BJ felt assured the boy would never pull a stunt like that again. BJ and Neil made the decision not to charge the parents with animal cruelty, even though legally they could have. It was, unfortunately, very uncommon that they ever located a perpetrator of such a random act of violence. It was one of the things that kept BJ going, not only finding out who was responsible, but also seeing they paid for their crime.

Neil smiled over at his partner as they climbed into the truck. He knew how happy she was with the outcome. It was the type of case they could close with a real sense of satisfaction.

"What do you say we stop and grab some lunch before we head over to speak to the..." Neil flipped open his notebook to double check the name Dr. Garrett had given them, "Quinns?"

"Sure thing. My treat. You can even pick the place."

Neil grinned. "All right!"

He happily headed for their favorite restaurant. He could already taste the deluxe Western Steak burger with the works.

* * *

"Mrs. Quinn?"

"Yes?" The woman stared suspiciously at the two uniformed officers standing outside her front door. She didn't recognize their uniform.

"I'm Officer Braden and this is my partner, Officer Martin. We're from the San Diego Animal Control office.

Mrs. Quinn frowned. "What can I do for you?"

"Your veterinarian, Dr. Garrett, contacted us about what happened to Blackie. She informed us that you and your husband have some concerns about the students from the school next door throwing things into your yard," BJ said.

Mrs. Quinn relaxed at the mention of Dr. Garrett. Tears sprang to her eyes at the thought of Blackie. "You think someone poisoned him? Dr. Garrett told us she treated him for rat poisoning."

"At this point, Ma'am, we don't know. It's possible someone in the area is having a rodent problem and didn't realize the effect using poisoned bait could have on other animals. We are checking all the yards around the school. We'd like your permission to examine your yard."

Mrs. Quinn nodded miserably. She hoped it had indeed been something accidental. It made her sick to think that someone would intentionally try to hurt Blackie. She led the officers into the backyard.

* * *

It was late when BJ and Neil headed back for the office. The search of the Quinns' yard had turned up nothing. They had found some rocks that matched the decorative rock used in the school yard. Mrs. Quinn claimed the school children frequently threw rocks at Blackie when he barked at them. The only other thing they had found was a few crushed soda cans that Mrs. Quinn confirmed were not left by her children. But there was nothing suspicious that would account for Blackie's symptoms. There turned out to be quite a few yards that bordered the school's property. It had taken quite some time to search those to which they had been able to obtain access. Unfortunately, the search of the other yards surrounding the school was just as fruitless.

So far, none of the neighbors they had questioned admitted to having a rodent problem or trying to poison them. Then again, when animal control officers showed up asking questions, it wasn't unusual for people to lie outright.

The last places they checked had been the Palmers and Mrs. Daily's yards. Although, neither one bordered the school yard they wanted check them for any signs of something that could have poisoned the dogs. Not wanting to upset the owner's in their grief unnecessarily they had simple said they were conducting an animal survey. Despite their recent losses, both owners had been extremely cooperative.

"Damn it!"

Neil jumped when BJ's fist hit the dash. "What?"

"I know we're missing something. The more I think about it, the more certain I am."

"We looked BJ. There wasn't anything there, no Rodenticide pellets, no animal droppings, no dead rodents, nothing."

BJ ran her fingers through her hair, making her already spiky hair stand straight up. "I know, but what if it wasn't an accident? What if the dogs didn't get into the poison pellets or chew on a poisoned rodent? What if someone intentionally baited those dogs?"

"That's pretty far fetched!" Neil said. "We didn't find any indication of anything out of the ordinary, even in the Quinns' yard where that was a possibility."

"I know. It's just..." BJ had no proof, but her instincts were screaming.

"It's much more likely someone is using poison and just doesn't want to admit it. Maybe they've heard about the dogs getting sick and are worried they will be held responsible. I think this is one of those cases we're just going to have to write off. We've got nothing."

BJ sighed in frustration. "You're probably right, but I think we should talk to Dr. Garrett again, as well as check and see if anyone else at the office has had any suspicious deaths of unknown etiology reported."

Neil knew the case for all intents and purposes was over. But what the hell, by indulging BJ he might get a chance to ask out the beautiful vet. He had thought of her striking gray eyes and curly dark hair frequently over the weekend. *Yeah, and maybe this time you'll get a glimpse under that lab coat.* He wished it had been him the lovely doctor had knocked down. Unlike BJ, he would have taken full advantage of the doctor sprawled out on top of him. Neil grinned at the thought.

"We can swing by there now and see Dr. Garrett, if you want."

BJ looked over at her partner in surprise, it was after six o'clock, and they were already on overtime. BJ knew how much he hated working overtime.

She smiled at Neil gratefully. "Thanks."

"Anytime."

CHAPTER 8

"$\mathcal{D}$R. GARRETT, THERE are two animal control officers out front asking for you," Barbara said.

The clinic was officially closed. Kody was finishing up the final evening check of all the in-house patients before heading home. Normally, she did the final checks by herself, but Dr. Donaldson had been hovering over everything she did all day.

Dr. Donaldson looked up from the cat they were checking and glared at Kody. "Get rid of them," he said, just loud enough for Kody to hear.

Kody glanced at the tech just in time to see the spiteful smirk on her face before she turned away. Kody ground her teeth. The spurned tech was doing everything she could think of to make Kody's life miserable. It was nothing she could call her outright on, but it was effective none the less. She knew all the techs must have heard Dr. Donaldson screaming at her this morning. Leave it up to Barbara to try and stir up trouble.

Barbara followed Kody back to the front desk and began fiddling with the computer system, shutting it down. Kody glared at the tech before turning her attention to the two officers. She wasn't sure what she was going to say. Although she knew she was right, she didn't want to lose her job.

BJ and Neil were waiting on the other side of the receptionist's desk. Emily had already left for the night, along with the other techs. It was Barbara's turn to lock up the clinic for the night.

BJ threw a quick glare at the tech who let them in. She had been incredibly rude. The door to the clinic had been locked when they arrived. The woman had at first refused to open it, pointing to the closed sign on the door with an arrogant smirk. BJ had insisted, pointing to her badge and the woman had finally relented.

BJ smiled at Kody when she stepped out from behind the tall receptionist's desk. "Sorry to come by so late, but we just got done checking out all the yards. We –"

"Umm... fine. Thanks for letting me know." Kody could feel eyes on her. She glanced over at Barbara, but the tech appeared engrossed in what she was doing. The feeling continued and she was willing to bet Dr. Donaldson was watching. "I appreciate you looking into it for me. I realize now I overreacted. I'm sorry I wasted your time."

BJ stared at Dr. Garrett, confused by her sudden change in behavior. The vet had specifically asked them to stop by and let her know what they had found and now she was blowing them off. It didn't make any sense. She managed to catch Dr. Garrett's eyes. BJ frowned when the woman cut her eyes to the side like she was trying to look behind her without turning around.

Stepping a bit to the side so she could see behind the doctor, she spotted a stocky man with wispy thin gray hair standing in the hallway. His large gut could be seen beneath his lab coat even from this distance. He was glaring daggers at the vet's back, but quickly stepped into an open door way in the hall when he realized she had seen him. BJ wondered if the man had anything to do with Dr. Garrett's abrupt attitude change.

"Well, sorry we couldn't be more helpful," BJ said, watching the doctor's face carefully.

Kody opened her mouth, then snapped it shut without saying a word. She wished she could explain to the officers what was going on. She looked over at BJ helplessly.

BJ was more convinced than ever that something had happened. She remembered Dr. Garrett had mentioned in passing on Saturday that the senior vet, who also happened to own the clinic, was due back today. She grinned when an idea struck her.

"Thanks for your time, Dr. Garrett. Come on, Neil. Let's head over to Salsa's. Remember, I promised you dinner," BJ said, all the while staring at Kody. The restaurant was only a few blocks from the clinic. BJ hoped the doctor was familiar with it and understood what she was trying to do.

Kody smiled and nodded slightly. The two officers turned and made their way out of the clinic.

* * *

"What the hell was that all about?" Neil asked as they headed back to their truck.

"Didn't you get it?"

"Get what?"

"Did you see that guy standing in the hall?"

"No."

"There was some guy, I'm assuming Dr. Garrett's boss standing in the hall. He was glaring at her while she was talking to us. He ducked into one of the rooms when he saw me. I bet he's why she changed her tune all the sudden and doesn't want to talk to us. You know how some vets are, they think we're the enemy and are trying to control their practice. I couldn't figure out why she kept trying to look behind her without turning her head 'til I spotted him."

"I'll be dammed," Neil said. "What was that bit about dinner?"

"Dr. Garrett is going to meet us at the restaurant."

"What... how can you be sure of that?"

BJ shrugged. "I just am. Look, if she doesn't show you get a free dinner out of the deal. Okay?"

Neil shook his head. What the heck, it was still work but if the beautiful vet did show up, who knew maybe he could get her phone number.

"Okay, you win. Let's go."

CHAPTER 9

NEIL AND BJ waited at the restaurant for almost thirty minutes. They were just getting ready to give up when the front door opened and BJ spotted Dr. Garrett. She grinned and waved her over to their table.

Both officers watched avidly as the doctor approached the booth. It was the first time either had seen her without her lab coat. Neither was disappointed with what they saw.

"Sorry it took so long. Dr. Donaldson, my boss, had to check every patient with me." Kody's irritation was apparent.

"Not a problem. Have a seat. We waited for you to order," Neil said with a charming smile. He slid over in the horse-shoe shaped booth forcing BJ to move so there was a space for Kody to slide in next to him. He was trying his best not to be obvious in his ogling, but it was hard; the vet's body was all he could have hoped for. He wondered what it would be like to run his hands over her lush, full breasts.

Kody hesitated, suddenly a bit nervous about this. She was going against her boss's direct orders, but wanted to know what, if anything, they had found.

BJ looked up at Kody and smiled brightly. "Come on, Doc, aren't you hungry? I'm starving. Let's eat. Then I'll fill you in on where we stand with the case."

Kody stared mesmerized for several moments into the woman's vivid green eyes. All her worries and concerns just seemed to evaporate. The waitress arriving with chips and salsa broke the spell. Laughing a bit self-consciously, she sat down next to Neil.

Everyone quickly placed their orders.

Neil looked between his partner and the beautiful vet, trying to figure out what he had seen just before the waitress arrived. It was as if the air had crackled between them for several seconds. He shook his head and laughed to himself. He must have just imagined it.

BJ was well aware of the strange connection she seemed to share with Dr. Garrett. Her gray eyes had changed color and become more blue than gray in the few seconds they had stared at each other. BJ was captivated to say the least. She was a bit taken aback by her strong reaction to the doctor. The vet's body was even more appealing than BJ had hoped. The great body she suspected lurked beneath the doctor's baggy lab coat was abundantly apparent beneath her tailored oxford shirt and chinos. A strong surge of arousal toward the vet made BJ tongue tied. It was very unusual for her to react so viscerally to someone. BJ wondered what it would be like to caress her voluptuous curves. *Down girl,* BJ ordered her seldom heard from libido. *You're starting to behave like Neil.*

While they waited for their food to arrive, Neil decided to try and get to know the lovely vet a bit better. They had agreed before Dr. Garrett arrived to wait until their meal was finished before getting down to business.

"So, have you been a vet for very long?" he asked.

Kody flushed, trying to quickly swallow the chip she had just bitten into. "Almost four years."

"It must be fascinating work. Did you start working for Dr. Donaldson right out of vet school?"

"No. I've only been working with him about eight months."

Neil had hoped to get the vet talking about herself. He draped his arm over the back of the booth behind Kody. Turning toward her slightly and smiling his most charming smile, he tried again to get her to open up. "Do you like being a vet? It must be very rewarding."

"Yes, I do," Kody said.

Neil was getting frustrated. He never had this much trouble getting a woman to talk to him. Usually by this point, they were babbling away about themselves.

BJ regarded Neil with growing anger at his obvious attempt to chat up Dr. Garrett. She was relieved when their food arrived.

Neil tried repeatedly during the meal to draw Kody out with little success. BJ struggled to hold back a satisfied smirk when she repeatedly gave him short, straightforward answers and nothing else. She sat quietly and ate her dinner, content to watch the doctor across the booth.

Kody was ill at ease given all the questions Neil was peppering her with. She had come here on business, not to socialize.

Kody looked over at BJ, then quickly away before she could lose herself in her eyes again. She just couldn't fathom her strong reaction to the woman; it just wasn't like her.

* * *

Kody got right down to business as soon as she finished her meal. "Well, I guess I should let you know what was going on at the clinic. I assume that's why you let me know where you were going for dinner."

At BJ and Neil's nods, she quickly explained what had happened that morning at the clinic.

"That bastard," BJ said, totally unaware that she had spoken aloud.

Kody laughed ruefully. "Well, as much as I tend to agree with you, the man is my boss. I just wanted to find out if you had found anything at the Quinns' and to apologize for how I treated you at the clinic."

BJ blushed when she realized she had spoken out loud. Although she could swear with the best of them she was usually very careful about her language while in uniform. But the thought of the other vet screaming at Dr. Garrett had just raised her hackles.

"We understand. Under the circumstances, you didn't have any choice. We didn't find anything suspicious at the Quinns or any of the other yards that bordered the school yard. There was also no evidence of Rodenticide or dead rodents. We found a few rocks that matched those in the adjoining school yard and a few crushed soda cans. Obviously the kids are throwing things at the dogs, but nothing that would support any of the dogs being poisoned," BJ said. "The Palmers' and Mrs. Daily's yard was clean as well."

"I'm relieved to hear that. I guess my boss was right after all." Kody sighed in frustration. "I was so sure..."

BJ opened her mouth to tell the vet about her theory, but Neil jumped in before she could speak.

"Just because we didn't find anything doesn't mean the animals weren't poisoned," Neil said. "It's not uncommon for people to lie to us. They fear they will be held responsible for what ever happened, so they just outright lie. It's also possible that the dogs were intentionally baited. In that case, it's unlikely we would find any of the poison lying around. Usually someone doing something of that sort uses a very small amount of hamburger or cheese, something most dogs would readily consume."

BJ looked over at Neil in surprise. In the truck on the way to the clinic, he had insisted her theory that the dogs were intentionally being poisoned was far fetched at best. Now he was espousing it as if it was his own idea.

Neil reached over and patted Kody's arm. "Don't worry. I'll keep after this and get to the bottom of it. I'm going to contact our fellow officers and see if anyone else has had any reported deaths of unknown origin."

Kody smiled brightly at Neil for the first time. "I really appreciate that. I hope it turns out to be nothing and that the cases are unrelated." She was happy and relieved to realize she wasn't alone in her suspicions or concerns.

"I'll take care of it, Dr. Garrett. I promise," Neil said.

BJ couldn't believe what Neil had just pulled. She felt a flash of totally irrational jealousy when the vet smiled at Neil and he reached out and touched her. She shook her head at the strange emotion.

"Thanks again." Kody glanced at her watch. "It's late. I should get going."

"Hey, Doc, how about some dessert? They make a great flan here," Neil said. He placed a gently restraining hand on Kody's arm, and then rubbed his hand lightly across her forearm.

Kody was uncomfortable with Neil's touch and pulled away. "Thanks, but I really can't stay. I need to get home to Jack."

BJ felt an immediate sense of disappointment. In retrospect, she shouldn't have been surprised that a woman as beautiful as Kody was already involved with someone. Although she didn't know if the vet was gay, she had, she now realized, harbored some hope that she might be. Her only consolation was the fact that Neil looked even more crushed at the revelation that Kody had someone waiting at home for her.

"He hates it when his dinner is late. Unfortunately for him, he can't open the bin where his food is," Kody continued, unaware of the reaction her comment had caused.

Seeing the confused looks on her dinner companion's faces, she laughed. "Jack... Blackjack, is my dog."

It was a toss up who was more relieved by the news, Neil or BJ.

BJ stood and so did Kody. Neil slid out of the booth after them.

"How much do I owe you?" Kody asked, stepping close to BJ when she saw the check in her hand.

"My treat, Dr. Garrett. I wish we could've been more help and I'm sorry we got you into trouble."

"Thanks, BJ, and it's Kody," she said, offering her hand.

This time BJ was prepared for the tingle that the vet's touch always seemed to evoke. She grinned when she saw Kody's eyes widen at the sensation.

Where Kody had been uncomfortable when Neil touched her, BJ's hand in hers felt like the most natural thing in the world.

"You're more than welcome," BJ said, momentarily losing sight of where she was as she continued to hold onto Kody's hand and stare into her eyes. She was fascinated as Kody's eyes changed color as she watched. She had never seen anything like it before.

"We'll get back to you as soon as we learn something new," Neil said. He didn't know what was happening between these two but he didn't like it. There was no way the beautiful vet was gay.

"Um... great... sure," Kody said. She felt an immediate loss when BJ suddenly released her hand.

"We probably shouldn't contact you at the clinic. Why don't you give me your home number and I'll call you," Neil said.

Kody looked over at the handsome blond, shifting uneasily. His earlier behavior had clued her in that he was interested in more than the case.

BJ stepped in to save Kody. She had seen the look in Neil's eyes and knew it well. It was the same look he had every time he chased a new conquest.

She drew her business card out of her pocket and quickly wrote a number on the back. "Here's my card. I put my cell number on the back. You can give me a call either at the office or call my cell if we're out in the field. I'll bring you up to date with any additional information we turn up. I would appreciate it if you'd call me if you have any more unexplained deaths or illnesses."

Kody smiled in gratitude. "Thanks, I'll give you a call in a couple of days to check in. If anything comes up at the clinic, I'll let you know immediately."

Neil glared at his partner. He had come so close to getting the vet's phone number. He figured after a few calls about the case, he could work in asking her out. She had finally seemed to be opening up to him a bit. He could still see the bright smile she had turned on him.

They walked Kody out to her truck before heading back to the office to pick up their own vehicles.

None of them noticed the dark figure watching from a car in the restaurant parking lot.

CHAPTER 10

BARBARA LOOKED up and grinned when she saw Dr. Donaldson enter the clinic. She volunteered to open the clinic today in hopes of catching him before Dr. Garrett arrived. After the fireworks between them yesterday, she had taken the chance that he would be working this morning, even though he usually didn't come in until later in the day.

"Good morning, Dr. Donaldson."

"Barbara," he acknowledged as he headed for his office.

"I just wanted to tell you how glad I am that you're back. The clinic really needs you. Things were just not the same while you were gone," Barbara said.

Dr. Donaldson stopped in his tracks and turned back toward the tech. "What do you mean? Did something happen that I don't know about?"

Barbara immediately began to backpedal. "No. I mean, you know what happened... It's just... well I don't like to speak badly of people. I'm sure she did the best she could."

"Who? Is there a problem with one of the other techs?"

Barbara looked down as if hesitant to speak, when in reality she was trying to hide her smirk. "I really shouldn't have said anything. I mean she's my boss too..."

"If you know something about Dr. Garrett, you need to tell me right now. Think about what's best for the clinic."

"Well..." Barbara pretended to hedge. "It's just that well, those two poor dogs. The first one, Missy, well I'm sure she tried her best to save her, but she just didn't seem to know what to do. I tried my best to help her, but she wouldn't listen to me. And the other one, poor Buddy, she didn't even try to save him. She just took one look and said, 'There's nothing I can do.' I mean she should have at least tried. I know you would have." Barbara gazed up at the doctor with a fake look of reverence. "I just know if you had been here, neither of those poor dogs would have died."

Dr. Donaldson's chest puffed out. "Yes, I'm sure I could have saved them. It's a shame. He stepped over closer to Barbara and patted her on the back. "You did the right thing telling me. I'll make sure I keep a close eye on Dr. Garrett."

Barbara watched as Dr. Donaldson headed for his office. Once he was out of sight, she smirked triumphantly. "Take that, bitch," she said. "You think I didn't see how you were looking at that glorified dog catcher. What's she got that I don't?"

* * *

BJ walked into the office and tossed several case folders on the desk.

"Good Morning," Neil said. BJ grunted in response. "No coffee this morning?"

"I didn't feel like stopping. Why don't you stop once in a while?"

Neil frowned up at his partner. It wasn't like BJ to be so surly. "Long night?"

BJ was still pissed off at the way Neil had acted last night. She could still see Kody smiling brightly up at him after he espoused her theory on what had happened to the dogs. Just the thought of them together made her jaw clench. It did not make any sense; she had no claim on Kody, but it bothered her nonetheless.

"What have we got on today," BJ asked, totally ignoring the question.

Neil started to press but the look on BJ's face quickly dissuaded him. "We have four new calls and two follow-ups. Two are homes we've been to before. Mr. Dudley has a new dog, and it's tied to the same doghouse where Muffy died."

"Shit! Who called it in?"

"Mrs. Bunch, same as last time."

"Okay, that's twice he broke the court order not to have any more dogs. Let's cut to the chase and get a warrant before we even go over there. I'm sure Judge Holden will be more than happy to sign it. He was pretty pissed last time Mr. Dudley violated his order." They had warned this guy repeatedly before they started more serious proceedings; BJ was sick of dealing with him. "Then we'll call Brian before we head over so he can meet us there." Brian was a San Diego police officer assigned as liaison to animal control to handle situations like this. "I'm sure he'll be more than happy to take Mr. Dudley downtown to get booked," BJ said with a satisfied smile.

"Okay, we'll take that first, and then tackle Mrs. Pulley."

BJ groaned. "Not again."

Neil laughed. "Yeah, her landlord called this time. His building maintenance man went in to unplug her toilet. He claims there are over thirty cats in the apartment again."

"Damn. I swear I coughed up hairballs for days after the last time. We better grab a bunch of extra crates before we head out. Maybe we should call Carl and see if he can give us a hand." BJ sighed; these repeat offenders were always difficult to deal with. "All right, let's do it."

"Oh, I almost forgot. I talked to Sharon and Raulo," Neil said, referring to their fellow animal control officers. "They're going to look over their back cases for any unexplained deaths that were never solved. I told them what was going on. Sharon said she'd talk to David and Wayne. I figured we could talk to Carl while he's giving us a hand with the cats."

"Good." BJ was pleased that Neil finally seemed to be taking her suspicions seriously.

"Yeah, I was thinking maybe, if we found anything, we could ask Kody out to dinner with us again," Neil said. "Just so we could let her know what was going on, as promised," he added quickly when BJ started to scowl.

BJ's anger rose when she realized what Neil was really interested in, and it wasn't the case. She should have known; so much for taking her concerns seriously.

"Leave her alone, Neil."

"What do you mean? I was just trying to keep our promise."

"Bullshit! You think I didn't know what you were trying to do last night. When chatting her up didn't work, you used the case." BJ batted her eyes and smiled broadly in a parody of Neil's attempt at flirting. "Don't worry, Dr. Garrett, I'll get to the bottom of this. I'll take care of it, I promise," she said, mimicking Neil. "You were ready to write this case off. You only got interested again when you thought it would help you get into Kody's pants." BJ slapped the desk angrily.

Neil was furious. He wasn't sure what made him madder, BJ's attitude or the fact that what she said had a grain of truth.

"Well, excuse me for trying to help. What's it to you if there's a little fringe benefit to this lousy job? You're not interested. What do you care?"

BJ glared at Neil. "I mean it, Neil. Keep it in your pants around Kody!"

Neil stared at BJ incredulously, then started to laugh. "You're interested in her, aren't you?"

BJ said nothing and continued to glare at Neil.

"Come on, BJ, give me a break. You can't seriously think someone like her could be gay. No way." He laughed outright at the very thought. Neil flinched at the look of pain that flashed across BJ's face.

"Oh, of course, Neil, how could I forget? Only pathetic butch women are gay 'cause they can't get a man. Right?"

"I... damn it; I didn't mean it like that. I just ..." Neil grimaced. That had been exactly what he thought, someone as beautiful as the vet couldn't possibly be gay.

"It doesn't matter, gay or straight, leave her alone."

Neil had never seen BJ act like this about anyone. "You're really serious?"

BJ stared hard at Neil. "Dead serious. Stay away from Kody."

For the first time in their five year partnership there was an underlying tension between them. It was going to be an uncomfortable day.

CHAPTER 11

KODY SMILED when she picked up the chart outside the door of her last appointment of the day. It had been a long miserable week and she couldn't wait to get out of here. David and Bobby were owned by a beautiful Siamese cat named Sheba. Her personality matched her name perfectly, she thought she was a queen and the two men her loyal servants.

The two boyishly handsome men looked up when Kody stepped into the room.

"Hey, Dr. G, how's it hanging?" David said.

Bobby elbowed his partner sharply in the ribs. David grinned unrepentantly.

Kody laughed. "Hey, you two. How's it going? How's business?"

Bobby and David where in their early thirties; both men were slim and extremely well built. They owned a local antique shop only a few blocks from the clinic. They were partners in every sense of the word, in their professional and personal life.

"We're doing good, girlfriend, and business has been great. Thanks for asking," Bobby said. His expression turned serious. "Unfortunately, our little girl isn't doing so well. She has those lesions again." Bobby looked down worriedly at the cat wrapped securely in his arms. "You haven't been feeling very good either, have you baby?" He stroked Sheba's fur gently.

Kody reached out and gently stroked Sheba's head. "Hey, sweet girl, are you worrying your daddies again?"

Sheba butted Kody's hand and meowed loudly as if refuting the statement.

"Come here, sweet baby." Kody lifted Sheba out of Bobby's arms and began to examine her gently. Sheba, true to the traits of her Siamese breed, could be extremely feisty and vocal if aroused. Kody always made a point of speaking softly to the very intelligent animal, telling it what she was doing as she worked. Both men watched anxiously.

Kody carefully separated a particularly nasty looking section of fur to see the skin underneath. The area immediately began to seep pus and bleed. Sheba let out a raspy meow in protest, but didn't try to get away from Kody.

"I'm sorry, sweetheart," she said to the cat as she reached for a gauze pad to press against the area.

She looked up in concern when she heard a loud groan. Bobby had buried his face in David's neck. He was the more sensitive of the two. David wrapped his arms around Bobby when his knees started to buckle.

Kody smiled understandingly at David as he comforted his partner. "I'll just take her into the back to finish my exam." It wasn't the first time Bobby had reacted poorly to Sheba being examined.

Bobby looked up and smiled sheepishly. "I'm okay."

David kept his arms securely wrapped around Bobby and motioned for Kody to continue.

Her examination finished, Kody settled Sheba comfortably in her arms. Sheba rubbed her head against Kody's chin.

"Well, the infection is back and worse than before." Her statement was greeted with two loud groans. "I know. I know. What I think we should do –"

The door to the exam room swung open and Dr. Donaldson strode in.

Kody ground her teeth. Dr. Donaldson had been shadowing her all week. He questioned every decision she made and barged in while she was examining patients. He had been showing up first thing in the morning and not leaving until the last patient had been seen. She had not been alone in the clinic since he returned on Monday. He normally didn't work at all on Friday, but here he was.

Dr. Donaldson glanced over at Bobby and David. A quick grimace of distaste crossed his face before he turned to Kody without even acknowledging their presence.

"What have we got here?"

Kody's anger soared at his rudeness. She had noticed before that he didn't seem comfortable with their more openly gay clients, which was ironic, considering the fact that his clinic was located in an increasing gay community.

"Mr. Higgins, Mr. Granger, this is my associate, Dr. Donaldson. He owns the clinic."

Both men nodded. David had seen the strained expression on Dr. Donaldson's face when he noticed their embrace. He couldn't resist tweaking the man. He winked at him and waved with a pronounced limp wrist.

Bobby rolled his eyes and scowled playfully at his partner. David batted his eyes innocently. Kody struggled not to laugh.

Dr. Donaldson took a step backwards and looked like he was going to bolt.

Kody growled under her breath at his unprofessional manner. Forcing herself to be calm, she addressed her boss. "Sheba is a five year old Siamese with a repeat skin infection of unknown origin. She originally presented with a skin infection four months ago. She was successfully treated with antibiotics at that time. Symptoms of the current infection appeared three days ago," Kody said. "I was just about to suggest we culture the lesions for bacterial type and drug sensitivity."

Without a word, Dr. Donaldson jerked Sheba from Kody's arms and plunked her down on the exam table. Sheba decided she didn't care for the doctor's bedside manner and made her displeasure known by sinking her rear claws into the man's restraining hands. He let out a loud yell and immediately released her. Sheba hissed at him before jumping off the table and scurrying to the nearest corner.

Bobby hurried to where the loudly meowing cat was cowering. He picked her up and cradled the outraged cat protectively to his chest.

Dr. Donaldson was furious; both hands were bleeding from multiple deep scratches. "That animal is dangerous. Why wasn't it muzzled? It should have been done from the start. I won't have my staff endangered by such a vicious animal."

He pulled a cat muzzle out of his lab coat pocket and stepped menacingly over toward Bobby.

"Don't touch her, you beast!" Bobby clutched Sheba tightly to his chest.

"That animal is dangerous," Dr. Donaldson said.

Kody moved forward quickly, blocking Dr. Donaldson's access to the frightened cat. "Sheba has never so much as hissed at me. I'll take care of her."

Dr. Donaldson spun on his heels and stomped over to the door. He turned back to glare at Kody. "I want to see you in my office as soon as you're through here." Without another word he exited the room and slammed the door behind him.

Kody turned to face David and Bobby. They were both huddled protectively around Sheba. Bobby had tears running down his face as he repeatedly stroked Sheba's fur murmuring to her softly. She reached out and squeezed Bobby's shoulder gently, and then rubbed his back soothingly trying to calm him.

"I'm so sorry about that."

"What's going on?" David asked. They had seen Kody several times and Dr. Donaldson had never come in before. They had never seen the man before except in passing. They had been clients of Dr. Ferguson, the vet who worked at the clinic before Kody.

Kody grimaced wondering just how much to tell them. Sighing, she decided after what had happened she owed them some type of explanation.

"Dr. Donaldson was gone last week and we had some very serious cases. When he got back he didn't agree with how I handled the situation, so he has been overseeing me all week." Kody knew that made her look bad but didn't feel comfortable airing her problems with her boss to a client. She looked at the two men sadly. "I understand perfectly if you would feel more comfortable taking Sheba to a different vet. I know several I can recommend. Again, I'm very sorry for what happened."

Kody started in surprise when both men embraced her. They had easily read between the lines of what she had told them.

"We're both very pleased with your care of Sheba and are fully confident in your abilities," David said. "We've both had to deal with asshole bosses. Don't you worry about it one bit."

Bobby nodded in agreement and Sheba let out a loud meow as if wanting to get in her two cents. Kody laughed in relief and smiled gratefully at the two men.

"Now what do you suggest we do for Sheba? You were going to tell us before we were so... rudely interrupted," Bobby said.

Kody explained what she had in mind. Both men readily agreed. After getting the necessary samples, she instructed them in what medication she wanted Sheba to take until the test came back. That settled, she sent them on their way with a promise to call with the test results as soon as they were available.

CHAPTER 12

KODY STARED down at the chart on her desk unseeingly. She had been trying unsuccessfully to finish up her paperwork but all she could hear were Dr. Donaldson's words reverberating in her head. She had found him in the treatment room after finishing up with Sheba. He was still ranting about vicious cats and the incompetence of today's young vets. Barbara, of all people was wrapping his scratched, bleeding hands and unsurprisingly egging on his anger. "In my office NOW! Garrett," he had snarled as soon as he saw her.

What followed had been a dressing down of epic proportions. Anything she had tried to say in her or Sheba's defense had just further fueled his anger. Kody had eventually just shut up and let him scream. He had detailed her every supposed short coming in the eight months she had been working at the clinic.

She shook her head in frustration. It was obviously time to start looking for a new job. It was a shame; she had really come to enjoy the varied clients and stimulating case load.

Just to top off her already rotten day, when she returned to the treatment room after Dr. Donaldson had finally run out of steam, all the techs suddenly appeared very busy. No one would meet her eyes, with one exception; Barbara had met her eyes evenly before looking away, but not before Kody had seen the satisfied smirk on her face.

"Dr. Garrett."

Kody jumped at the unexpected voice. She turned in her chair to find Andrea standing in the doorway of her office.

"Come on in."

Andrea stepped into the small office. Kody's eyebrow quirked when she shut the door behind her.

Andrea looked over at Blackjack's empty blanket. "I really miss the big guy. How's he doing?"

"He's fine. A bit put out being left at home alone, but he'll survive."

Andrea shuffled her feet and looked extremely uncomfortable. She would not meet Kody's eyes.

Kody waited several moments for the tech to speak up. When it became obvious that Andrea wasn't going to tell her what was on her mind, she stood up, then sat on the edge of her desk, facing the tech. "What's wrong?" she asked in a gentle voice.

Andrea took a sudden interest in the tops of her shoes. "I umm... I just wanted to say... umm..." She stopped and took a deep breath then finally looked up and met Kody's eyes. "I...I mean the techs and I wanted you to know that we think you're a great vet and that Dr. Donaldson is being very unfair to you." Andrea blushed vividly but didn't look away.

Kody smiled warmly. "Thanks. I really appreciate that, but it might be better for all of you if you kept that opinion to yourselves. I don't want any of you to get in trouble on my account; he does own the clinic."

"But it's not right, Dr. Garrett! Someone should say something to him."

Kody reached out and placed a calming hand on Andrea's shoulder. "I know, but there's nothing I can do about it right now. I'd be very unhappy if any of you were to get involved in this. Please just let it go."

Andrea started to protest but saw the determined light in Kody's eyes and desisted. Her shoulders slumped visibly. "Okay, but just know that all of us support you."

"Thank you; tell everyone for me that I appreciate it very much. But, I don't want anyone to approach Dr. Donaldson," Kody added, her expression stern until Andrea nodded in acceptance. Kody smiled warmly at the tech. "You closing up tonight?"

"No, Barbara is."

Kody tried not to grimace at the mention of the tech's name. Andrea said all the techs supported her; she very much doubted that included Barbara. Forcing a smile onto her face, Kody thanked the tech again and sent her on her way.

* * *

Barbara stood just outside Kody's door. She was happy to be able to observe the vet without her big brute of a dog warning the woman of her presence. Dr. Garrett had brought the dog in today, but took him home at lunch time after Dr. Donaldson made a big fuss.

She had decided that now that the haughty vet had been taken down a peg or two she would give her a second chance. Barbara knew that they would make an incredible couple if the woman would just see how much she had to offer.

Kody shifted, suddenly conscious of being observed. She quickly turned in her chair to find Barbara standing just outside her door. She stood and walked over to face the tech.

"Yes, what can I do for you?" Kody tried her best to keep her tone professional despite her dislike of the tech.

Barbara grinned lasciviously. She would love to tell the vet just what she could do for her and where. At Kody's scowl, the grin quickly dropped from her face.

"I just wanted to let you know everything is secured for the night."

"Thank you. I'll be ready to leave in just a few minutes."

Kody turned without another word and started to put the charts away. She gathered up her things and moved back toward her office door. She pulled up short when she realized Barbara was still standing there.

"Yes?" Kody asked, trying to keep her temper when she noticed where the tech's eyes were.

Barbara pulled herself out of her fantasy; she had been so busy perusing the good doctor's body she hadn't realized the vet had spoken.

Barbara smiled up into Kody's eyes and took a step closer to her, well into her personal space. "I know a great Chinese place not far from here; let's go get some dinner."

Kody scowled. *Not this again!* She thought she had been very clear the last time the woman asked her out. "No," Kody said firmly and clearly before turning to walk away. She gasped in shock when Barbara grabbed her arm and spun her back around.

"What's your problem? You think you're too good to be seen with a tech? Well, Miss High and Mighty, Donaldson didn't seem to think too much of you today, did he?" Barbara sneered. "It's just a lousy meal. What's the big fucking deal?"

"Take your hand off me, NOW!"

Barbara flinched at the blazing anger on Kody's face and quickly removed her hand.

Kody's hands clenched into fists; she couldn't believe this woman's audacity. She took several deep breaths to calm herself.

She glared down at the diminutive blond. "I've tried to be polite, but you just don't seem to get it. I'm not interested in seeing you or anyone else I work with outside of this clinic. Don't ask me again." Kody stepped around Barbara and started to walk away.

"Well, that sure didn't seem to be the case the other night," Barbara said. "I'm sure Donaldson would love to know who you had dinner with on Monday."

Kody stopped dead in her tracks. How the hell does she know about that?

She turned to find Barbara staring at her triumphantly. Kody stood rooted to the spot as Barbara approached and once again stepped into her personal space.

"But it could just be our little secret." Barbara smiled warmly at Kody. "Come on, let's go get our dinner," she said as if the previous conversation had never happened.

Kody was floored; she couldn't believe the little bitch had the gall to try and blackmail her! She took a step away from the tech, her eyes turning stormy gray and burning with anger.

"You do whatever you think you have to, Barbara," Kody said before turning and storming away. She ignored the repeated calls of the irate tech.

* * *

Barbara stood frozen for several moments after Kody's abrupt departure. Finally, her temper exploded and she slammed her fist into the wall.

"You'll be sorry, bitch! You just wait. You'll be sorry you ever fucked with me!"

She stomped into the treatment room. One of the dogs barked as she passed its crate. She viciously kicked the crate door. "Shut up, you stupid mutt."

After kicking several more cages, she gained some control of herself and completed locking up the clinic. Barbara muttered to herself as she made her way to her car, "Yeah, you'll be sorry, bitch. You're just like all the rest. You think you're so superior. Well, we'll just see about that."

CHAPTER 13

"*I* THINK YOU better take a look at this."

BJ looked up in surprise. It was Friday and Neil was always hot to leave and start his weekend. He had left almost a half an hour ago. "What's going on? I thought you went home."

"Raulo stopped me on the way out." Neil handed BJ a sheaf of papers. "You were right, just look at these."

BJ quickly shuffled through the reports, her eyes widening the further she read. "Holy shit! These are all confirmed?"

"Yeah, as much as they could be, without a necropsy it's a process of elimination but they sure as hell fit what we've been seeing. Sharon is still looking for reports to see if there are any that slipped through as unknowns."

BJ continued to flip through the papers. "These go back over three years!"

"Look at how they're clustered, that can't be an accident," Neil said.

This past week had been stressful for both of them; after their argument on Tuesday the atmosphere between them had remained strained.

Neil shifted uncomfortably. "Listen, BJ, I owe you an apology. You were right about this case all along."

BJ shrugged. "Forget it. It's not about us; it's about protecting the animals."

Neil put his hand on BJ's shoulder. "No, I mean it. You were right about me. I did think the case was a waste of time and I used it as a way to try and get close to Dr. Garrett. I'm sorry. I don't want this to come between us. We're too good a team."

BJ didn't know what to say. She had rarely heard Neil apologize and when he did it was usually just a half assed attempt.

She hated the tension between them all week but had been very hurt by his comments and didn't quite know how to get past them.

Neil squirmed at BJ's continued silence. Knowing the tension between them was mostly his fault and cursing his big mouth he knew what he had to do.

"And umm... I'm sorry about the other... I mean umm... If you're interested, you should ask Kody out." Neil was confident that the beautiful vet wasn't gay. Let her be the one to shoot BJ down.

BJ shook her head in amazement; she couldn't believe what she had just heard. She stood up and pulled a surprised Neil into a hug. "Apology accepted. And I'm sorry I came on so strong about the whole thing. I just..." BJ shrugged, unable to explain it, even to herself. "What do you say we grab some dinner, my treat?"

"What about all that?" Neil asked pointing to the reports on the desk.

"I'll take them home and go over everything this weekend. It'll still be here on Monday. These are all old cases, not anything we can really do at this point. Let's get something to eat. I'm starving."

Neil couldn't hide his surprise. He had expected BJ to want to dive right into the reports. "Can we go to Hooters?" he asked, wiggling his eyebrows.

BJ laughed heartily, happy that the tension between them had eased. "Don't push your luck!"

Neil stuck out his lip in a fake pout then laughed. "Come on, partner, I'm starving."

CHAPTER 14

𝒦ODY HAD BEEN debating for the last hour about calling BJ. She had originally intended to call her last night after work but had been too upset about the confrontation with Barbara. Now, she was unsure if she should call her on a Saturday, maybe she should wait until Monday.

She picked up the business card on the table. "Oh, what the hell." Picking up the phone determinedly, she quickly dialed BJ's cell phone number before she could change her mind.

"This is Officer Braden. How may I help you?"

Kody froze for a second when she heard BJ's crisp professional greeting. She thought the number was BJ's personal one. She had no way of knowing that the only calls BJ got even on her cell phone were work related.

"Hello?"

"Hi... umm..." Kody cursed under her breath. She took a deep breath to regain her composure. "This is Dr. Garrett."

BJ smiled brightly when she realized who was calling. "Hey, Doc. How's it going?"

Kody smiled at the sudden warmth in BJ's voice. "Good, thanks. I just wanted to check in with you about the case."

"Have you had any more problems at the clinic?"

"No, no more suspicious cases have come in."

"That's good news. We did finally turn up something at the office." BJ briefly explained about the reports her fellow officers had compiled, not wanting to go into too much detail while using a cell phone.

"Son of a bitch!" Kody blushed when she realized what she had said. "Sorry. I just... I can't believe it."

BJ chuckled. "No worries. I felt the same way."

"Would it be possible to see the incident reports?" Kody was curious now that her suspicions had been confirmed. And maybe, just maybe, there was something she could do to help. The thought that someone was intentionally harming animals infuriated her.

BJ was more than willing to meet with the vet, regardless of the reason. She had thought a lot about her all week, although, she did feel a bit guilty about seeing Kody without Neil. She knew how he would see it when he found out, especially since she had insisted Kody was off limits. Pushing away the distracting thoughts, she decided for once to follow her heart's urging.

"Sure, no problem. How about we meet somewhere for lunch?"

Barbara's words suddenly echoed in Kody's head and she hesitated.

BJ caught the hesitation and wondered if she had over stepped and seemed too eager to see the vet.

"Or you could stop by our office on Monday," BJ said.

Kody really wished she could talk to someone about Barbara. Maybe BJ would understand; she was pretty sure the woman was gay. But you just never knew for sure. She **had** thought a lot about the handsome officer all week.

"Lunch would be good, but umm... would you mind coming over here to my place?"

BJ's eyebrows shot up in shock. Did she hear what she just thought she heard?

Kody sighed in regret when BJ didn't respond immediately. "Or I could just drop by the office on Monday."

"No, I'm off today, so lunch would be great. Give me directions and let me know what time to – DAMN!"

"What's wrong?" Kody became concerned when she heard rustling and then what sounded like a growl of pain. "BJ! Are you all right?"

BJ came back on the line, slightly short of breath. "Sorry about that. I'm fine."

"What happened? Are you sure you're all right?"

BJ was embarrassed and really didn't want to explain. BJ sighed and faced the inevitable; she was never going to live this down. "I brought home two young pups from work that are being bottle fed. When you called I had just started feeding them. They were lying on my chest, and I guess I got a little distracted..."

"And?" Kody said when no further explanation seemed forthcoming.

"One of the bottles slipped... and one of the pups dug their claws in and umm... grabbed something else instead."

It took Kody several seconds to get it, and then she roared with laughter. "Let me guess... you don't have a bra on?" As soon as the words left Kody's mouth she felt a strong flash of arousal at the thought.

BJ groaned in mortification. She had intentionally left that little detail out.

Kody tried to get her laughter under control. "I'm sorry... I know it's not funny. It must have really hurt."

"Nah. I'm all right just shocked me mostly." Quickly getting back to the topic at hand, she asked, "What time should I be at your place? I can't stay too long 'cause of the pups."

"What feeding schedule are they on?"

"Every three to four hours. It was a long night last night."

"Well, if you're too tired..." Kody's disappointment was obvious.

"No! I'm fine, really," BJ said.

Kody chuckled. Obviously she wasn't the only one looking forward to this. She didn't know what it was about BJ but she felt drawn to her. It didn't make any sense – she barely knew the woman.

"Why don't you bring them with you? I'd be happy to give you a hand."

"Really?" BJ said. Kody took care of animals all day; she was pleasantly surprised that she would offer to help on her off time.

"Sure, it'll be fun."

"What about Blackjack? How is he with other animals?"

Kody laughed. "Don't worry. He's wonderful with other animals, especially baby animals. He has pretty much grown up in vet clinics, and is used to all sorts of animals. Speaking of Jack, you don't mind big dogs, do you?"

"Ah, Doc, I'm an animal control officer. Remember?"

"I know that! Even some vets aren't comfortable around all breeds of dogs." She couldn't help thinking of Dr. Donaldson and his adamant dislike of giant breed dogs. "Blackjack is a Great Dane. And what's this Doc stuff? I thought we agreed it was Kody."

BJ smiled. "Right... Kody it is. And I love big dogs."

"Great, cause he's definitely big." Kody said. "It's nine thirty now, so how about noon? That way I can give a hand with the pups next feeding.

"I'll see you then," BJ said.

CHAPTER 15

*B*J HAD BEEN sitting in her truck outside Kody's house for the last ten minutes trying to work up the nerve to go up to the door. She had suffered several minutes of total panic about what to wear after hanging up the phone with Kody. After having a good laugh at herself, she dressed in her usual jeans and a tee shirt. BJ wiped her sweaty palms on her pants. *This is ridiculous. Pull yourself together woman! This isn't a date.* Thus mentally fortified, BJ grabbed the carrier with the two puppies inside and made her way to Kody's front door.

* * *

Kody jumped when the doorbell rang. After completing the call with BJ she had raced through the house trying to make sure it was presentable, even going so far as to change the sheets on her bed. She had been halfway done when the absurdity of the whole thing struck her – like there was any possibility BJ would be anywhere near her bed.

A quick check of the kitchen had revealed how bare her refrigerator was necessitating a quick trip to the grocery store. She had just finished getting everything ready when the doorbell rang.

Kody gulped when the bell rang again and Blackjack's bark echoed from the patio. She quickly hurried to the door.

"Hi."

BJ stared, once again struck by the beauty of the woman before her. She was dressed in jeans and a tee shirt as well. "Umm... hi," she stammered, then cursed herself.

Somehow BJ's obvious nervousness made Kody feel better. "Come on in."

BJ followed Kody into the living room and set the carrier with the pups down next to a large, overstuffed, comfortable looking couch that dominated the room. A strange sound made her turn and look toward the dining table and chairs that sat in the far corner of the room.

BJ spotted a forlorn face staring in through the glass patio door in the dining room. "I take it that's Blackjack? He's beautiful."

Kody looked over and laughed. "Thanks." Blackjack started to wag his tail frantically and let out a loud "woo woo" sound when he noticed his master's regard. "He's trying hard to be good. He doesn't much care to be outside alone."

"Let him in."

"Are you sure? I know he doesn't look it, but he's still fairly young. I'm working on his training. He does pretty well in public, but he tends to be rather rambunctious on his own turf especially if he thinks you like him."

BJ walked over to the sliding glass door. Putting her hand on the knob, she quirked an eyebrow at Kody questioningly.

Kody quickly joined her. "Umm...maybe you better let me get a leash on him. He really doesn't have a clue how big he is. Why don't you have a seat?" Kody indicated one of the chairs at the square butcher-block table.

"You worry too much; I do work with animals all day," BJ said as she reached out and slid open the door.

Before Kody could say anything else, Blackjack barreled in. He jumped around trying to greet both women at the same time.

BJ laughed and tried to pet the whirling dervish. "Hey there, big guy. Let me get a look at you."

His shoulder slammed into BJ's thighs, knocking her off balance.

"Blackjack! NO!" Kody said as the big dog jumped up and placed both big feet on BJ's chest. Kody grabbed his collar, but it was too late. Already off balance, BJ went down. Blackjack managed to jump clear, but jerked Kody off her feet. She let go of his collar and fell, sprawled on top of BJ.

BJ's breath left in a whoosh as Kody landed on top of her. She looked up into Kody's startled face and laughed.

"Seems we've been here before." BJ smirked. "We have to stop meeting like..." She looked up into Kody's eyes and totally lost her train of thought.

Kody looked down into BJ's eyes and froze. All rational thought flew from her brain. She lost herself in the emerald depths below her. Everything seemed to recede except those stunning eyes drawing her closer. The air seemed to crackle between them. Kody licked her suddenly dry lips and her eyes flickered down to BJ's lips. She wondered what they would taste like. She unconsciously moved slightly forward.

Blackjack chose that moment to make sure his owner was all right. He poked his muzzle into Kody's back making her jump.

Kody realized she had been seconds away from kissing BJ. Becoming aware of the intimacy of their position, she blushed fiercely. Rolling off of BJ, she quickly regained her feet. "I'm so sorry. Are you all right?"

BJ felt an irrational sense of disappointment when Kody moved off her. "I'm fine," she said, getting up off the floor and rubbing the back of her head.

"Are you sure you're all right?" Kody asked worriedly. She stepped close to BJ and ran her hand up the back of her neck and into her hair, feeling for damage.

Kody's touch sent a shiver of pleasure down BJ's spine. She was much more aware of the feel of Kody's breast pressed against her arm than any pain from her head.

Kody could feel a small bump on the back of BJ's head, but there didn't seem to be any serious damage. Still, she was angry at Blackjack; he knew better than to jump on people.

"You've got a small lump here, but it doesn't seem to be bleeding or ..." The crackling energy that had sparked between them a few moments ago returned. Kody's hand, seemingly of its own accord, slid from the back of BJ's head around to cup her face. Their lips were inches apart...

Blackjack's insistent presence intruded again, pushing between the two women and startling them apart. The interruption brought Kody back to her senses. She realized just how seriously BJ could have been injured.

Kody moved away from BJ and rounded on Blackjack. "Bad dog! You know better than that! You can just stay outside." She grabbed his collar intent on putting him out.

Kody jumped when a hand covered hers. "Wait. It wasn't his fault. You did try to warn me. No harm done – really. Let him stay." BJ was perturbed with Blackjack, but not for knocking her down. She was sure Kody had been about to kiss her and would have if he hadn't pushed between them. "Please," she added with an adorable smile.

Kody let go of Jack's collar and gently squeezed the hand still around hers. "Are you sure you're really okay?"

"Scout's honor."

Kody laughed and looked down at Jack when he licked her hand contritely. "You are so lucky. Go get in your bed," she said.

He quickly made his way over to the large foam bed in the corner and lay down dejectedly.

"How about I grab us a snack and something to drink? What would you like?" Kody asked, returning her attention to BJ.

"Iced tea, if you have it."

"Have a seat and I'll be right back."

* * *

BJ took a deep breath and sat down on the couch; she was shaking. She was stunned that she and the beautiful vet had almost kissed twice in just a matter of minutes. Another second and she would have accepted the open invitation on Kody's face and tasted her lips. She wasn't sure what had happened. One second she had been laughing over the accident and enjoying the feel of Kody's body pressed close to hers, then one look into warm eyes and she had been lost. In seconds, Kody's eyes had gone from gray to the most incredible shade of blue BJ had ever seen. She wanted to drown in them. She swore she could still feel Kody's soft body pressed to hers. *Damn, get a grip! You barely know the woman.*

She had been sure Kody was going to kiss her when she cupped her face with her hand. The heat from Kody's palm had seemed to radiate from her face and settle around her heart. She sent a disgruntled look over at Blackjack where he lay quietly in his bed.

She knew it wasn't the big dog's fault, but couldn't help wishing that he had waited just a few more seconds before interrupting them.

BJ shifted and grimaced when she felt how wet she was. *Oh great, that's all I need. How am I going to behave myself around her if with just a look, she can get me wet and throbbing?*

The two pups she brought with her began to cry; it was their feeding time. Forcing her thoughts away from the woman in the next room, BJ turned her attention to her charges.

* * *

Kody gripped the counter in agitation; she didn't know what was the matter with her. She had never reacted to anyone quite so viscerally before. *Another second and you would have kissed her.* All she could think about was the feel of BJ's hard body under her and how much she wanted to feel it again, minus the clothes this time. Kody shook her head, trying to force away the erotic images that thought inspired. *This is nuts, I don't sleep with women I barely know.* But the temptation to do just that was almost overwhelming.

Not finding any ready answers for her unusual reactions, Kody turned her attention to pouring up two glasses of tea. She pulled out the cheese and crackers she had made earlier as well. Taking a calming breath, she headed back into the living room.

* * *

Kody smiled when she spotted the two yellow balls of fur in BJ's lap that were each sucking on a finger. *Lucky little buggers.* A warm blush covered her cheeks at the thought.

"What happened to their mom?" Kody asked, trying to take her mind off what seemed to be up most in her thoughts – BJ.

"We don't know. About three weeks ago, we got a call from a woman who said she heard crying when she was taking out her trash. She had put her trashcan out the night before and was just adding a bag to it. When she lifted the lid the crying got louder. She found six puppies in a paper bag inside the can. The vet said they were a day or two old. These two are the only ones that survived, and even they aren't out of the woods yet."

Kody shook her head in disgust. She had seen abused animals before, but she normally dealt with people who cared about their animals enough to bring them in to see her.

"I take it you never found the culprit?"

"No. We canvassed the area but never found anyone whose dog had recently had puppies or at least anyone we could get to admit to it. Someone most likely knew enough not to dump them in their own neighborhood. If they had just brought them to the shelter we would have taken them and even help them get the mom spayed. It's just such a waste," BJ said. She smiled when Kody sat down next to her and patted her arm. "Sorry. I tend to get a bit passionate about animals being abused."

"Nothing to apologize for. I think we should treat the owners in exactly the same manner as they treat the animals. See how they like being chained outside in all kinds of weather and starved or beaten," Kody said.

BJ's eyebrows rose in surprise. She felt the same way but was surprised to hear Kody verbalize the same feelings. Trying to lighten the mood, BJ held out one of the squirming pups to Kody. "Want to give me a hand feeding them?" She leaned down and pulled two bottles from the carrier and put them on the coffee table.

Kody took the pup and cuddled it close to her breast. It wasn't much bigger than her hand.

BJ smirked and waggled her eyebrows at Kody.

Kody looked down to where the pup was rubbing its face and blushed. She mock scowled at BJ.

"Well, at least I'm wearing a bra. Are you?" Kody asked, her eyes immediately going to BJ's chest. She blushed vividly at her own boldness.

BJ looked shocked for a second, and then laughed hysterically at the sight of Kody's bright red face.

"Want to see for yourself?" BJ asked, her hand beginning to pull her tee shirt out of her pants.

Kody's eyes widened; the strong flash of arousal was immediate. She bit her lip, her eyes going back to BJ's chest. Kody did the only safe thing. She grabbed the bottles and fled into the kitchen.

BJ's laughter followed her hasty departure.

* * *

BJ looked over where Kody sat cross legged on the far side of the couch. She had a pup cradled in her arm and was stroking it gently. BJ couldn't help smiling at the contented look on her face. They had talked of inconsequential things and enjoyed their iced tea and snack while they fed the pups. BJ looked around when she heard a high-pitched whine that hadn't come from either of the pups.

Kody knew exactly where the sound was coming from. She looked over at Blackjack.

"Okay, come on, you big baby."

BJ laughed when she realized who had made the noise. She grinned when he gently nuzzled the tiny puppy in Kody's hand. He stepped over and carefully sniffed the puppy BJ held out to him, and then licked BJ's face before she could react.

Laughing, she wiped her spit covered face on her shirt. "Thanks, big guy. I like you too."

Kody reached out to pull Jack away. He lay down on the floor, between the two women.

"He's fine. Not the first time I've been covered in dog spit. Though I will give him credit, he can cover a lot of territory with that tongue," BJ said.

Kody's mind jumped into the gutter and heat flashed through her body. She would love the chance to show BJ just how much territory her tongue would like to cover. *What is wrong with me? I don't think that kind of thing.* She reminded herself that BJ was here on business.

"Did you bring those reports with you?" Kody asked, forcing a professional expression on her face.

BJ blinked at the rapid change in Kody's demeanor. She wasn't quite sure what she had seen on Kody's face. She had looked... enthralled and then her expression had gone blank. BJ was disappointed; she was enjoying their time together. It had been a long time since she had just spent time with a woman, especially someone like Kody. She wasn't looking forward to talking business, especially the kind of business this was about.

"Sure. Just give me a minute to get these guys settled." BJ reached down and placed the sleeping puppy into the carrier then took the second puppy from Kody's arms and put it next to its littermate in the nest of warm towels lining the bottom of the carrier. She pulled a folder out of the back of the carrier before closing the door.

Kody had seen the flash of what looked like disappointment cross BJ's face and felt bad. It wasn't her fault Kody couldn't control herself.

Kody smiled. "What do you say we have some lunch first? I picked up turkey breast, roast beef and some pastrami, oh and a couple of great cheeses for sandwiches. I've got potato salad, macaroni salad, and pasta salad." Kody stopped when she spotted the grin on BJ's face. "I wasn't sure what you liked," she said with a shy blush.

BJ stepped close to Kody. "You didn't have to go to all that trouble for me."

Kody swallowed nervously at BJ's proximity. "I wanted to."

BJ took a step back before she could give into temptation. "Thank you. Show me the way and I'll give you a hand with lunch."

CHAPTER 16

"*T*HAT WAS GREAT," BJ said, patting her stomach.

Kody smiled. "Glad you liked it. Are you sure you wouldn't like something else?"

BJ looked at the food containers spread all over the table. She had already had second helpings of everything.

"No thanks. I'm stuffed. Anymore and you'll have to roll me out the door."

Kody couldn't believe how easy it was to talk to BJ. They had continued to talk about their interests; movies they had seen, music they liked and a whole host of other things. Surprisingly, the one thing neither of them had mentioned was work. They had yet to look at the reports BJ brought.

Knowing she couldn't put it off forever, and that it was the reason BJ was sitting at her table, Kody turned her attention to business.

"Let me clear this mess away and we can take a look at those reports."

BJ was disappointed, but knew that Kody was right. She had been having such a good time that, for a little while, she had forgotten her purpose for coming over in the first place.

* * *

Kody stared at BJ in shock. It was much worse than she thought. "Oh my god! These reports go back over three years."

"Right. And not only that, but each occurrence is clustered around a few blocks of a neighborhood. That's one of the reasons a red flag didn't go up before now. There were four or five cases in each area all confined to a small radius, then nothing. Then six months later, it's a new area. Again, just a few cases, then nothing. By themselves, it would seem to point toward an accidental poisoning. A simple case of someone in the area was treating their yard and adjacent dogs got poisoned. That does happen, but not with this frequency."

BJ reached out and gently squeezed Kody's arm in understanding at the growing look of dismay on her face. She had been appalled that morning when she realized the scope of what they were facing. It just proved once again how understaffed they were for the size of the city they were asked to police. This should have been caught much sooner.

"That's not all. The other strange thing is that different animal control teams cover each of these areas. So no single officer was responsible for investigating more than one group of these cases. If they had it might have alerted us to what was really happening. Not to mention the fact that except in Pacific Beach none of the reported cases were filed by a vet or vet clinic. The vet there contacted us after having five cases all come to his clinic within a week's time. All the other calls came from individuals whose dogs were effected. While investigating that person's complaint, the other cases in that neighborhood were found, which again added to the perception that it was an isolated incident. So no one noticed a pattern until you brought it to our attention and we specifically started looking for one."

BJ stacked the reports into five piles. "See... these occurred in Pacific Beach, Scripps Ranch, South Bay, Del Mar and then these last ones, near your clinic in North Park. These clusters occur six months apart from the last poisoning 'til the first one in the new area, except for the ones at your clinic. The last poisoning in Del Mar was eight months ago, so it's a larger time gap than previously."

"Why would someone do this?" Kody said. She couldn't help thinking of the defenseless animals that had died.

"I don't know. But I'm damned well going to find out."

"Is there anything I can do?"

"No. Not right now, but I appreciate the offer. Just keep your eyes open and let me know if you see any animal with suspicious symptoms in the clinic. You've already done more than you realize by bringing this to Animal Control's attention." BJ smiled gratefully at Kody. "Who knows how much longer it would have gone on?

Now that we know these cases are not accidental, we have a chance of catching whoever is doing this."

"I'll let you know right away. I'm also going to talk to Andrea, one of my techs. I know she's trustworthy and will let me know if any animal comes in while I'm not there."

"Still having trouble with your boss?"

"You have no idea," Kody said. She wondered if she should confide in BJ about what was going on.

BJ's watch beeped loudly interrupting. "Oh, damn. Sorry."

"What's wrong?"

"I didn't realize it'd gotten so late. The pups are going to need to be fed again in a half an hour."

"That's no problem. I enjoyed helping," Kody said with a warm smile. She was more than happy to help with the puppies and it would give her a chance to discuss her situation at work with BJ. She felt confident the woman would understand and be sympathetic. Maybe she would have some good ideas on how to handle Barbara. Kody knew she obviously hadn't been doing a very good job so far.

"It's not that. I only brought them one bottle each." BJ cursed her oversight. She glanced over at Kody and noted her disappointed expression. BJ felt a bit better knowing she wasn't the only one who didn't want to see their time together end.

Kody stood up reluctantly. "I guess you should get going then." Kody put Blackjack out in the backyard before following BJ to the door. "Oh, before I forget I wanted to give you my number." Kody pulled a business card out of her pocket and handed it to BJ.

"I've got the clinic numbers," BJ said.

"Yeah... I umm..." Kody reached out and flipped the card over. "That's the number here and my cell. I meant to give it to you last week..." Kody wasn't sure how to explain. She had been hesitant to give her home phone number out while Neil was present. His interest had been very clear. She didn't want to be the cause of any problems between the two partners but didn't feel comfortable with Neil having her home phone number.

BJ seemed to read her thoughts. "Not a problem. I won't give it to anyone else."

"Thanks."

They stared at each other awkwardly, neither quite knowing what to say. A car door slamming nearby broke the standoff.

"I should go. Thank you for lunch."

"You're very welcome."

Kody stood by helplessly as BJ turned to walk away. *Say something stupid!*

"BJ."

BJ quickly turned back to face Kody.

"I umm... I know you came over to bring the reports, but I really had a good time today, despite what brought you here. Thanks for bringing the puppies. And I'm really sorry about Blackjack knocking you down."

BJ stepped back toward Kody. Without even thinking about it, she reached out and clasped Kody's hand. She smiled at the now familiar tingling of her fingers.

"I had a good time too. Blackjack's just a big lovable boy. Don't worry about it. He didn't hurt me, honest."

Kody lost herself in BJ's emerald eyes. Whatever it was between them sparked anew.

BJ's breath hitched as Kody's eyes turned blue. She unconsciously stepped closer and entwined her fingers with Kody's. Nothing existed except Kody's face in front of her. BJ's gaze narrowed down to Kody's lips and she shifted forward to answer their call. Their lips were inches apart when the carrier in her free hand banged against their legs breaking the spell.

BJ stepped back and shook her head. *What the hell was that!* She looked at Kody and saw the flush on her face and the rapid beating of the pulse in her neck. She wanted so much to just give in to the pull of those eyes and kiss her but berated herself for the impulse. She was here on business. "I um... guess I better go." The cries from inside the carrier reinforced her words.

Kody blinked several times. Her mind was trying to catch up with her body. She had totally lost touch with her surroundings when BJ leaned close. Finally, pulling herself out of the sensual haze she had fallen into, she smiled at BJ.

"I'll call you in a few days to see if you've learned anything more... if that's okay?" Kody said.

BJ grinned. "It's more than okay. Call anytime."

They stared at each other for several moments before another more strident cry from the carrier forced BJ on her way.

CHAPTER 17

KODY PULLED into the parking lot at the back of the vet clinic and sighed in relief. Dr. Donaldson's car was not in the lot. She normally worked alone on Monday and Friday. She knew Barbara had been scheduled to work on Saturday with Dr. Donaldson. Kody couldn't help worrying that the tech had followed through with her threat to inform her boss that she had met with the animal control officers after he had expressly forbidden it. At this point, she wouldn't put anything past the spurned tech. Hopefully, after the fiasco on Friday with Sheba and her owners, her boss would leave her and her patients alone. She could only hope that was the case and that Barbara's threat was an empty one.

She was also anxious to see what, if anything, had happened in the clinic on Saturday because of the information BJ had given her. Her normal days off were Wednesday and Saturday. Dr. Donaldson worked alone in the clinic on those days. The clinic was closed on Sunday. She was worried additional cases might have come in while she was off; she knew Dr. Donaldson wouldn't report them.

Kody grabbed her briefcase out of the passenger's seat before getting out to lock up her vehicle. She started in surprise when the back door of the vet clinic opened. Tom, the young vet tech who worked nights when they needed him quickly exited. He disappeared around the corner of the building before she could call to him from across the parking lot.

Kody hurriedly made her way toward the clinic, after seeing Tom she was concerned. He only came in if they had a serious case requiring around-the-clock care. It was strange for him to leave before one of the tech's came in to relieve him. She jumped and spun around when a car horn sounded behind her. Lisa pulled into the space next to her truck.

Lisa rushed out of her vehicle and ran across to where Kody stood outside the back door of the clinic.

"Sorry I'm late, Dr. Garrett."

One of the tech's was assigned on a rotating basis to arrive a half an hour before the clinic opened to unlock and get everything ready for the day ahead.

Kody glanced at her watch and smiled. "You're not late, I'm early. I wanted to get caught up on some of my paper work."

Lisa pulled out her keys and unlocked the door. Kody did have her own set of keys to the clinic so she could come and go as necessary.

"So what case came in on Saturday that Tom got called in?" Kody asked worriedly. She knew Lisa had been the other tech working this past Saturday.

Lisa turned and looked at Kody blankly. "Tom? He wasn't working that I know of. Saturday was really quiet, just a few routine things – well puppy examinations, vaccinations, that kind of thing."

Not wanting to arouse the tech's suspicions, Kody smiled and brushed the comment off. "Oh, I must have gotten confused. If you need me, I'll be in my office." *What the hell was he doing here then?* she wondered as she made her way to her office.

* * *

BJ slapped the dash in frustration. "Damn it! Nothing." In addition to their regular calls they had spend the week doing some follow ups on what they now knew were intentional poisoning cases.

"We knew it was a long shot to start with," Neil said. "Any clues would be long gone, not to mention as we saw most of the people don't even live in the same place anymore."

They had gone up to Del Mar in hopes of following up with the last group of people who had animals die before the current cases in North Park. Only one person still lived at the address they had. Two of the families had been military and been transferred and the third had moved to Oregon.

"So what... We just sit on our hands 'til they strike again and more dogs die!" BJ said.

"I agree with you; it's frustrating, but what else can we do?"

BJ blew out an exasperated breath. "I know, you're right... I just..."

Neil glanced over when his partner fell silent. He knew how much this case was haunting her.

"Hey, have you heard anything from that vet, Dr. Garrett?"

BJ looked at Neil suspiciously. It was the first time all week he had mentioned Kody. She never had told him that she had seen her last weekend.

"Why?"

"We wouldn't have known what was going on without her help. I just thought she might appreciate knowing that she was right. And it might be worth checking that there have been no more cases in this group."

"She already knows," BJ said.

"When did you talk to her?" Neil still hoped to have a chance with the beautiful vet.

BJ shifted uncomfortably. She knew how Neil was going to react. She momentarily considered lying but knew he would eventually find out the truth.

"She called me on Saturday and I brought her up to date on what we'd uncovered. She wanted to see the reports so wehadlunchtogether," BJ said.

"What was that last part?"

BJ sighed. "We had lunch together."

"Well, thanks a lot – partner. I really appreciate you inviting me along. When were you planning on telling me?"

"Look, Neil, it wasn't like that. She called and I told her about the cases. She asked to see the incident reports. I took two young pups home with me last weekend. She invited me to lunch and offered to help me feed the pups. We fed the pups, had lunch, and went over the reports, and then I left."

Neil scowled at his partner. "You could have invited me."

"It was just a spur of the moment thing. It was no big deal."

Even as she said it, BJ knew it wasn't true. There had been more to it than that. The attraction she felt toward Kody was undeniable. She had jumped at the chance to see Kody alone and never considered including Neil.

"Wait a minute..." Neil glared at his partner as the significance of what she said dawned on him. "Where exactly did you have lunch?"

BJ cringed internally. "At her place."

Neil jerked the wheel in anger and the truck swerved into the next lane. The blaring of a car horn startled them both. Neil swung back into his own lane, then flipped off the driver who had honked at him.

"Have you seen her again?"

"No," BJ said, then wanting to be completely honest added, "I called her on Wednesday to let her know we hadn't had any luck so far with follow-ups."

"I thought we weren't supposed to call her at the clinic."

Shit! "I umm... called her at home."

"You have her phone number too!"

"Yeah."

Neil threw one last glare at BJ before returning his attention back to the freeway. He never said another word all the way back to their home base.

* * *

"Hey Doc."

Kody turned in her chair and smiled at Andrea. "All set?"

"Yes. We don't have any animals in house except the two cats that are being boarded. I checked them and they're fine."

"Just let me sign off on these charts and wake up the lump, then I'll walk out with you."

Andrea smiled down at Blackjack; he was sprawled out on his side sound asleep. "He had a tough day today."

Kody laughed. It had been a quiet day, especially for a Friday. Dr. Donaldson had finally stopped dogging her every step. She was happy to be back to working alone two days a week. After the other vet had not shown on Monday, she had taken a chance and brought

Blackjack with her today. Knowing the techs would keep an eye on him when she was busy, she had given the big dog the run of the clinic. He had played with every animal he could and approached every client that seemed responsive. In short, he had worn himself out.

Even Barbara had been on her best behavior; she had barely spoken to Kody all week, but had been polite and professional during their few interactions. Kody hoped that the woman had finally gotten a clue and the problems with her were behind her.

She had spoken to BJ on Wednesday and although there had been no progress on the case, there had been no further poisonings either. All in all it had been a good week.

Kody would only later realize that it was the proverbial calm before the storm.

CHAPTER 18

NO ONE THOUGHT anything about the stranger walking the Labrador Retriever down the street on an early Monday afternoon. Most of the people in the neighborhood worked and it was pretty deserted during the day, but come afternoon it wasn't unusual to see someone out walking their dog. Many of the homes in the area were rentals with frequent tenant changes so it was not uncommon to see people in the neighborhood that you didn't recognize.

"This is going to be so good...yes it is," the stranger said to the furry companion.

Checking to make sure no one was nearby, the interloper slipped between two houses and approached the first fence, having checked out the area previously to know exactly where a dog was in residence.

A beagle ran up to the fence, wagging its tail and baying loudly.

"Shh...quiet now." The intruder urged the lab forward to sniff noses through the fence with the beagle. "That's right...play nice and I'll give you a special treat."

The trespasser reached into a backpack and pulled out a plastic bag filled with individually wrapped cheese balls. One of the cheese balls was offered to the beagle who gulped it eagerly and begged for another. The poisoner grinned and held out a second piece.

"That's right. Good boy. Eat it all gone. All gone," the killer said in an eerie voice as the dog eagerly swallowed the deadly treat.

Quickly putting the rest of the tainted cheese away the intruder looked around carefully before heading back to the sidewalk with the Labrador in tow.

The killer smirked in satisfaction. "One down – five to go." It was all too easy. *Wish I could be there to see all hell break loose.*

* * *

Kody jumped in surprise when Mike came barreling into her office. She had been catching up on her paperwork. It had been fairly quiet all day, especially for a Monday.

"We need you out front, right now!" He turned quickly on his heels and hurried back toward the lobby.

Kody had never known the former marine to be anything but calm, no matter what the situation. She rushed for the door, pushing Blackjack back when he tried to follow.

"Stay here, boy," she said and quickly closed the door.

She raced to the front of the clinic and skidded to a halt frozen in place momentarily by the sight before her. Standing in the middle of the lobby was Mr. Alton, a client of the clinic, who was bleeding from a bite on his forearm. More shocking was Rowdy, his Beagle. He was wedged between the couch and the wall, snarling at any movement and biting at himself. She had seen Rowdy for a routine office visit a few months ago. The Beagle had been gentle and as docile as could be. Quickly regaining her composure she took charge.

"Lisa, get me a towel for Mr. Alton's arm. Mike, go in the back and get both sets of heavy gloves and a thick blanket. Everyone stay back from the dog." Kody didn't want to do anything until she had an idea what she was dealing with. Thankfully, being late in the day, no other clients were in the lobby.

Lisa quickly provided the requested towel and Kody gently wrapped it around Mr. Alton's arm trying to stop the bleeding. He had not said a word since she arrived.

"Can you tell me what happened?" Kody asked.

Mr. Alton stared at Rowdy then down at his arm before turning to face Kody.

"I came home and Rowdy was acting very strange. He was racing around the back yard as if the devil himself were after him. I called and called to him but he wouldn't stop. Then he started biting himself. I didn't know what to do." Mr. Alton's voice broke as he relived those horrible moments.

Kody could see the dog had inflicted several wounds on itself. He seemed to have calmed down a bit so she took a cautious step toward the dog, and then quickly stepped back when he lunged at her.

Mr. Alton grabbed her arm. "Be careful. He'll bite you."

"Then what happened?"

"I didn't know what else to do. I got a big comforter off my bed and threw it over him as he ran past. He went crazy and started struggling. I finally got him wrapped up and he seemed to calm down a little bit. I brought him right over." He looked down at his arm a bit ruefully. "I thought he was okay. He seemed to be pretty calm when I got into the lobby so I uncovered him. As soon as his head was free he went crazy and started snarling, and then he bit me." His shock at his dog's behavior was obvious. "What's wrong with him?"

"That's what I need to find out. I'll need to get him sedated so I can take a look at those wounds and then see if I can figure out what is going on."

Kody turned to Lisa who had been watching from behind the counter. "I want you to clear everyone out of the back. Make sure all animals are secured in crates. I don't want anyone out. Pad one of the small crates with several blankets then draw up 2 ml of Acepromazine and have it ready for me. Let me know when you're ready."

Mike was standing by with the items Kody had requested. He donned a pair of the gloves. Kody turned to Mike and took the second pair of gloves. She took a step toward Rowdy, then hesitated. His owner didn't need to see this.

Kody put her hand on Mr. Alton's shoulder and gently guided him toward the door. "We can take it from here. You need to get to the hospital and have that arm looked at."

He looked back over his shoulder at the growling Beagle. "But Rowdy..."

"We'll take good care of him. You've done everything you can for him. Let me help now."

With gentle insistence Kody finally got him out the door. She walked back over to Mike and donned the second pair of gloves.

"You ready for this?"

Mike glanced at Rowdy and nodded. "What do you want me to do?"

"You take one side of the blanket and I'll take the other. I want to get it over his head as quickly as possible. It should be easier given how he's wedged in there and really doesn't have any where to go. I'll take control of the head; you get the rest of his body. Once we have him under control, I'll sedate him. Then we'll put him in a crate and wait for it to take effect."

"Everything is ready in the back," Lisa said from her safe spot behind the counter. She held the syringe with the sedative in it out to Kody.

"Okay, Mike... let's do this."

They approached the dog cautiously and quickly got it under control, thankful that they were dealing with a twenty-five pound Beagle and not something larger. Kody breathed a sigh of relief when they got him sedated and in a crate. She had no way of knowing that this was just the beginning.

CHAPTER 19

BJ FLINCHED when the dog slammed itself against the sliding glass door. They had gotten an emergency call from dispatch. A woman had called and stated her German Shepherd was trying to kill her. A San Diego Police Officer had arrived and checked out the situation before allowing her and Neil to enter the house. You never knew what you were walking into in this type of situation.

"I don't think we have any choice," Neil said. "I don't think a dart is going to do a thing."

The owner stared at the two officers trying to hear what they were saying, then looked out at her beloved Shepherd. King had always been a loving, gentle companion. She had come home from work to find him running frantically around the yard. When she called to him, he had stopped in his tracks in the middle of the yard and snarled, then charged. She barely had time to slam the sliding glass door before he hit it full force. He had thrown himself at the door repeatedly growling and biting at the door handle.

BJ looked over at the distraught owner. "Ma'am, you need to go outside with Officer Blake. She motioned for the SDPD Officer. "Please take her down a couple of houses." Blake nodded his head sadly; he had seen these situations before. It was a regrettable part of the job, but with an animal this size they really didn't have any choice. Their duty was to protect the public and not to get bitten in the process.

"Wait, please. What are you going to do?" the woman asked.

Neil stepped over. "Please go with the Officer, Ma'am, and let us do our job."

Officer Blake gently led the protesting woman away. As soon as they were sure she was clear BJ headed over to the large duffle bag with their gear.

Neil immediately protested when she pulled out the tranquilizer rifle. "That's not going to work."

BJ never looked up from her preparations. "We have to try."

* * *

BJ jumped startled from her thoughts by the squawking radio. They had just gotten into the truck to head back to the station. "Now what?" she said.

It had gone exactly as Neil predicted. He had managed to get two darts into the dog. One should have been enough, but it definitely should have dropped immediately after the second one. There had been enough drugs in that dart to take down a dog five times its size. The Shepherd had not even flinched and if anything had become more aggressive. When it had leaped at the fence where Neil was standing she had fired two shots from her nine millimeter. Though she understood she'd had no choice, the death of the dog had still affected her deeply.

"Go ahead, Dispatch," BJ said.

"We've got a priority call for you from a Dr. Garrett. She's requesting you meet her at her clinic in North Park as soon as possible."

"Did she say what it was about?"

"She said to tell you 'It's happening again'. Said you'd know what it meant."

This day just keeps getting better and better. Keying the mike, she said, "Thanks, Dispatch. We're on our way there now."

BJ had turned off her cell phone while they were dealing with the Shepherd. She turned it on as they headed for the vet clinic and listened to two agitated requests from Kody to call her.

* * *

Kody sat absently stroking Blackjack's big head. She had retreated to her office to try and get her emotions under control. She always strived to maintain her professional demeanor in front of the techs, never letting on how she really felt until she was home, alone. But this time she had almost lost it; she had never felt so helpless in her life. Rowdy turned out to be just the start of the nightmare that was to follow. They had barely gotten Rowdy situated when Mrs. Smith had arrived sobbing hysterically with Dancer wrapped in a blanket. She had found him with bite marks all over his hind quarters, lying in the bushes next to the house. There was nothing Kody could do; the little dog was already dead.

It was less than an hour later when the next dog came in. The dog wasn't a patient of the clinic. According to the owner, he had rushed home from work after a frantic call from his daughter. She claimed their Poodle, Fluffy had tried to bite her and was acting strangely running around the house biting at the air and herself. He'd gotten home to find his daughter barricaded in her room and the dog running around the house frantically. He'd been shocked when the elderly dog had charged him and tried to bite him on the leg. He managed to wrap her in a blanket and rushed her to the nearest clinic.

Both Fluffy and Rowdy had presented as if they were on some kind of high. The stress of what ever was effecting them had been too much for Fluffy's body to handle. The elderly dog had gone into convulsions and died shortly after arriving at the clinic. Thankfully, Rowdy was still alive, although she had been forced to sedate him a second time with a much heavier dose than normally would be required for a dog of his weight.

After Dancer's owner left Kody checked both Rowdy's and Dancer's chart. Her heart sank when she realized they lived on the same street. Kody had immediately tried to call BJ. After taking care of the Poodle, she had been almost afraid to check the owner's address. Sure enough, the Poodle's owner lived only one street over from the previous two dogs. She knew someone was poisoning these dogs, but she had no idea with what. She still hadn't heard back from BJ and had tried to call her again, only to once again get her voice mail. At that point, Kody had decided to call animal control directly. Kody sent up a silent prayer that no more dogs would come in tonight before wearily heading back to check on her patient.

* * *

"Dr. Garrett, there's someone here to see you," Lisa said.

Kody's heart raced. *Now what?* She looked back over her shoulder at the tech. An unconscious sigh of relief escaped when she spotted BJ and Neil.

"Hey, Doc," BJ said. Kody was kneeling in front of a blanket draped crate. BJ stared at her worriedly; she looked wrung out.

Kody stood and with one look into BJ's eyes knew something was wrong. Her eyes were dull and she barely managed a smile. "Is everything all right... Are you all right?" she asked, unconsciously stepping closer.

BJ shrugged. "Long day."

Kody was embarrassed to feel her eyes tearing up. "Yeah, I hear that." She brushed at her eyes impatiently.

BJ's concern ratcheted up another notch. "What's going on? I'm sorry I didn't return your calls. We had a... situation and I had my phone off.

Kody filled BJ and Neil in on what had been happening. She couldn't help the renewed tears that threatened to fall when she got to the part about the little Jack Russell terrier.

"Oh, Kody. I'm so sorry. Wait... Dancer. Wasn't that the little dog you were chasing the night we met?"

Kody nodded miserably.

BJ's insides clenched at the thought of the death of the feisty terrier. She wanted so badly to take Kody into her arms and offer what comfort she could, but she knew this was not the time or the place.

"Damn it," Neil said. "This sounds exactly like what happened with the Shepherd."

"What Shepherd?" Kody asked.

Before either of them could respond, Mike rushed into the treatment area. "I think we've got another case. Owner just came in."

Kody felt a rush of anger. *Not again!*

They all quickly headed for the front of the clinic.

* * *

Kody felt sick to her stomach when she spotted Kris Rawlings standing in the lobby. She had seen Willy for a few minor ailments since that day almost eight months ago. She had only been working at the clinic for a few days when the woman appeared with a dirty, emaciated, Great Dane in tow. She had rescued the dog from the freeway.

"What's going on, Ms. Rawlings?"

Kris felt some of her panic subside with the appearance of the vet. She had come to trust Dr. Garrett and knew she could figure out what was wrong with Willy if anyone could.

"I'm not really sure. I was at my condo picking up some files and had Willy with me. I let him out on the patio. He seemed perfectly fine. When I was done I put him back in my truck and headed home. About half way there he started acting really strangely, whimpering, and then growling. I pulled over to check on him and he cowered in the back of the truck. His whole body was shaking and he was unresponsive to me. When I tried to touch him he growled and snapped. It was like he wasn't even seeing me."

"Where is he now?" BJ asked.

Kris looked at the woman standing next to Dr. Garrett; her eyebrow arched in surprise when she noticed the uniform and realized she was an animal control officer.

"He's in my truck," Kris said, then turned back to Kody. "What's going on, Dr. Garrett?"

"We need to get him in the clinic and sedated," Kody said. Kris started to question her, but Kody quickly cut her off. "I'll explain everything as soon as I can, but right now our priority is Willy."

* * *

BJ and Neil followed Kody and Mike as the dog owner led them toward her vehicle.

Willy was curled up in a ball against the middle seat in Kris's SUV. He lifted his head and growled when the hatch swung open.

"Son of a bitch," Neil said. The dog was huge. He knew if it charged it could seriously injure one of them before they could stop it. "I'll get our gear."

Kris watched as the officer went over to the animal control vehicle parked nearby and returned with a large duffle bag. He opened the bag and reached in. At the sight of the weapon she stepped protectively between Neil and Willy.

"No... wait, Neil," BJ said. She had already seen one dog die tonight, there wasn't going to be a second if she could possibly avoid it.

Kody wasn't sure how they were going to manage this. Willy had filled out in the intervening months and was a very large, muscular, Great Dane. It was not going to be like subduing the Beagle or the Poodle was earlier. This dog could do major damage with a single bite. Willy had always been extremely docile when she had dealt with him previously. It was shocking to hear the gentle dog growling menacingly.

"What do you think, BJ, should I try to sedate him here or wait until we get him into the clinic?" Kody asked, eyeing the big dog nervously.

They had a heavy blanket and both she and Mike had donned heavy, metal lined gloves that extended up to their elbows. She also had a syringe filled with a tranquilizer.

"Give me the blanket and gloves, I'll get hold of him," Kris said.

BJ knew having the owner around while trying to deal with an animal was never a good idea. They tended to get hysterical and make her job harder.

"Ma'am, it would be best if you went inside and let us handle this. It's our job to deal with aggressive animals."

"Willy's not aggressive; he's sick. If you think I'm going to walk away and let you do anything you want to my dog," Kris glared at Neil before turning back to glower at BJ, "think again."

BJ growled under her breath. "Look, lady..."

Kody grimaced at Kris's and BJ's aggressive stances realizing that things could quickly get ugly. She stepped in and took charge. "Let's everyone calm down. We all want Willy to get the care he needs." Kody turned to BJ. "Do you think you could get a control stick on him?"

BJ started to order the owner away but a warning look from Kody stopped her. She eyed the situation, considering. "Yeah, that might work. If you close the hatch, I can open the rear door enough to get the stick in. Once I have the noose on him, I should be able to pin him against the seat. From there you can open the hatch again and use the blanket to cover his head. I recommend you give him the sedative out here, then once he's out we can get him inside."

Kris was still blocking the hatch to her truck and glaring at the two animal control officers. Kody walked over and laid a gentle hand on her shoulder. "No one wants to hurt Willy. Everything will be okay."

Kris subsided and with a sigh, turned and softly closed the back of the truck.

* * *

Kody rubbed her temples trying to push away a pounding headache. It was late, almost ten o'clock. They had gotten Willy subdued and settled into a large kennel in the back. He'd seemed fine and had surprisingly taken less of a dose of sedative than the beagle had. After BJ had questioned Kris extensively Kody had explained what she thought was going on. She had finally managed to convince Kris there was nothing else she could do and to go home to her family. Before BJ or Neil had a chance to bring her up to date on what had transpired with the German Shepherd they had encountered, Mike had rushed in to tell her that Willy was having a seizure.

Her heart sank when she reached the dog; his big body was contorted by the spasms. It had been touch and go for quite some time, but she felt confident that he had come through the worst of it.

She had insisted Mike go home over an hour ago, leaving her alone in the clinic. BJ and Neil had left while she was struggling to save Willy. She'd found a note on her desk from BJ. They'd had to leave to take the Shepherd from earlier to Animal Control. She smiled when she thought of the short P.S. to the note asking her to call BJ's cell as soon as she finished up, no matter how late.

"Hey, Doc."

Kody jumped at the unexpected voice. She still couldn't help wondering what he had been doing in the clinic last Monday before it opened. "Hi, Tom. Sorry to call you in so late."

"Not a problem. Mike filled me in. That must have really been something. Sounded like all hell broke loose. What do you think is going on? Who's doing this?"

Kody frowned and rubbed her hands over her face. "I'm not sure."

Tom seemed eager to question Kody further, but subsided when she refused to speculate. "You look beat; you should get some rest. I'll take over from here."

"Call me if there's any problem."

"You know I will."

Kody checked on the two dogs one last time before wearily heading home with Blackjack.

CHAPTER 20

Kody jumped when Blackjack growled a warning. She had been so engrossed in her thoughts she had lost track of her surroundings. Glancing around to see what had made Jack growl, her heart started to race when she spotted the figure lurking on her porch, not six feet away. Once again cursing her house's lack of adequate security lighting, she took a firm hold on Jack's collar and started to back away.

"Hey, it's me."

Jack woo woo'd as BJ stepped down from the porch and approached.

"What are you doing here?" Kody asked a bit more sharply than intended. Even as she said it, Kody regretted her tone; it was her fear talking. She didn't care why: she was just happy BJ was here.

"I um..." That's the question isn't it? What the hell are you doing here?

Now that Kody was here, BJ was in full panic mode. She really didn't know why she had come. After dropping off the Shepherd's body and explaining to the on-duty tech what needed to be done in the morning, she had headed home. She wasn't even aware of where she was going until she turned onto Kody's street, ending up in front of her house. Several times before Kody arrived home she had tried to convince herself to leave, but had remained nevertheless.

"I um... It's late. I shouldn't have come. I mean... um... You must be tired," BJ said.

"Never mind. Come inside," Kody said. She moved toward BJ, closing the small distance between them. She looked into BJ's eyes and then reached out for her hand. "I'm sorry I was so short with you. I guess all this going on with the poisonings has me kind of spooked. I'm glad you're here."

A bright smile flashed across BJ's face. "Really?"

Kody grinned. "Really. Now come inside. Jack's hungry and so am I and I know you must be too."

BJ entwined her fingers with Kody's and immediately felt a release of some of the day's tension.

* * *

"Want another beer?" Kody called from the kitchen doorway.

BJ jumped at the sound of Kody's voice. Kody had insisted she remove her gear and take off her boots, then left her comfortably ensconced on her sofa with a beer while she went to change her clothes, and then feed Blackjack. All the turmoil from earlier was, for the moment, gone. She had been content to drink her beer and relax while she waited for Kody.

"Sounds good." BJ picked up her empty bottle and started to get up.

"Stay right there. I'll get it."

"You don't have to serve me. I know you had as tough a day as I did."

Kody winced at the mention of work.

"Sorry," BJ said. Work was the last thing she wanted to think about.

"No problem. I just don't... I can't yet..." Kody choked up just thinking about the animals at the clinic.

BJ nodded. "Yeah, me either."

"So was that a yes to another beer?" Kody asked quickly dropping the subject.

"Sure."

Kody disappeared into the kitchen and returned with two beers.

BJ was pleasantly surprised when Kody sat down on the center cushion next to her and handed her a beer.

"Here's to better days," Kody said, holding up her bottle toward BJ.

BJ smiled and clinked bottles. "Amen to that!"

"Pizza should be ready in about fifteen minutes. Hope you don't mind frozen?" BJ's stomach growled loudly at the mention of food. Kody's eyebrow arched and she reached over and playfully patted BJ's stomach. "Soon – food is coming – soon."

BJ laughed. It felt so good to be here with Kody. It was as if all the cares in the world just faded away when she was with her.

Both women were content to just bask in each others company. Conversation wasn't necessary; it was enough to have the other nearby.

* * *

BJ sighed in satisfaction as she finished her last bite of pizza, and then followed it up with a swig of beer. She sat her beer bottle down and smiled at Kody.

"Thanks. That really hit the spot."

"No big deal, just a frozen pizza." Kody hesitated, then fortified by the two beers she'd consumed managed to work up her courage. "Maybe I could cook a real meal for you sometime?"

All right! "That would be great."

"It's a date then," Kody said a bit nervously, hoping that BJ had understood that she was asking her for a date. It had been a very long time since she had asked a woman out, and Kody was pretty rusty.

"Definitely," BJ said. "You tell me when and what time and I'll be here."

"Great." Kody blew out a breath in relief and then blushed when BJ grinned. She glanced over at the clock and groaned when she realized it was after midnight.

"Are you working tomorrow?"

BJ noticed Kody's look at the clock and was surprised how late it was. "Yeah, I am. I should probably get going." Though the truth was the last thing she wanted to do was leave. She wasn't looking forward to a long, lonely night in her apartment, especially with all that had happened.

"Are you okay to drive?"

BJ looked confused for a second, then smiled, when she realized what had Kody worried. "Well, just for future reference, you know in case you want to get me drunk and take advantage of me." BJ waggled her eyebrows at Kody, and then laughed when she blushed. "It takes more than two beers to get me buzzed, especially after all the pizza. I'm good to go. Seriously though, I appreciate the concern."

Kody was loath to ruin the lighthearted mood that prevailed but knew they needed to talk before BJ left.

"I hate to bring it up, but we should talk about what happened today. Before I got involved with Willy, Neil mentioned something about a Shepherd you'd had a problem with. Was it anything like the other dogs I saw at the clinic? What did your vets do to treat it?"

BJ felt her throat tighten at the mention of the Shepard. In all her time with Animal Control it was the first time she had ever fired a lethal weapon in the line of duty. She mentally squared her shoulders, and then began to tell Kody about their encounter with the German Shepherd.

BJ's eyes filled with tears as she told Kody of being forced to kill the Shepard. She brushed them away impatiently, determined not to break down in front of Kody.

"There was nothing I could do. I couldn't let him attack Neil."

"Oh, BJ. I had no idea. I'm so sorry."

One look into Kody's sympathetic gray eyes and BJ lost it. Before she could stop herself she began to cry.

Kody's heart broke for what BJ had been compelled to do. Kody dealt with animals that she was unable to help and had to be euthanized. It was an unpleasant but necessary part of her job, however she had always consoled herself with the fact that she was able to humanly and painless ease their suffering. She could not imagine being forced into a situation where the only option was to have to shoot an animal. She knew BJ had no choice, but it had still been an emotionally wrenching experience.

Kody wrapped her arms around BJ and pulled her to her chest. "It's all right. Let it all out." Kody's tears joined BJ's as the horrors of the day once again played through her mind. She stroked BJ's back and murmured softly to her as BJ began to sob in earnest.

CHAPTER 21

Kody gazed at the sleeping figure on her couch and smiled. BJ was curled up facing the back of the couch. She had held BJ last night until her tears had subsided and the woman fell asleep. She hadn't had the heart to wake her. The blanket Kody had spread over her was pulled up tight around her shoulders and all that was showing was the back of her head.

With one last glance at the sleeping officer, she headed for the kitchen to make coffee. She wasn't sure what time BJ had to be at work.

* * *

Kody was just picking up the pot to pour two cups of coffee when she heard a yelp, followed by a loud thud. She quickly ran into the living room and skidded to a halt in surprise. She didn't know whether to laugh or yell. BJ was on the floor in front of the couch with Jack standing over her determinately trying to lick her face. Her laughter finally got the better of her as she hurried over to pull Blackjack away.

"Come on, you big moose. No one appreciates dog breath this early in the morning." Having successfully subdued Blackjack she turned back to BJ to find her glaring at the dog from the floor.

"What happened?" Kody asked as she helped BJ up. She had a good idea, but she wasn't about to say anything.

BJ spared the big dog one last glare as she got to her feet. Her thoughts were still a bit jumbled from her abrupt awakening. She wasn't sure what time it was or how she ended up asleep on Kody's couch.

"I was just starting to wake up when I felt this warm breath on the back of my neck." BJ didn't add that at first she thought it was Kody nuzzling her neck. That was what made what she did find that much more shocking. "I turned over and came nose to nose with HIM," she glared over at Blackjack, who did his best to look innocent, "then he stuck his tongue in my mouth! That's when I fell off the couch."

"I'm sorry, BJ," Kody said struggling to control her mirth. She flinched when BJ glowered at her. "He really likes you and just gets carried away sometimes. And he's really sorry. Aren't you, Jack?"

Blackjack whined pitifully and his tail thumped on the floor. It was obvious he was struggling to stay on his bed where Kody had exiled him.

BJ mock scowled. "Well, while I might like to be woken up with a French kiss, it certainly wouldn't be one from him."

Kody laughed. "I'm with you on that one. I've had several from him and they did nothing for me either, except to make me want to run for my toothbrush." Kody relaxed when BJ laughed good-naturedly. "I was just getting ready to pour us some coffee when Jack decided to be your wake up call. Have a seat while I make us some bagels and grab the coffee. I wasn't sure what time you had to be to work."

"Need a hand?"

"Na, it will just take a few minutes."

* * *

BJ flopped back down on the couch, then glanced at her watch. "What the..." Still a little unsettled from her abrupt awakening she tried to remember what had happened last night and why she was still at Kody's house at seven o'clock in the morning. Her face reddened and she buried her face in her hands as the memories came flooding back.

BJ didn't know what happened, one minute she was explaining what she had been forced to do, and the next when she looked up into Kody's sympathetic eyes she had burst into tears. It was as if a huge barrier had been breached and it just all came pouring out – all the pain she buried on a daily basis. She had sobbed in Kody's arms, crying for all the animals she saw battered and abused. After that, things got a bit fuzzy and the next thing she remembered was waking up to Blackjack's big hairy face.

Feeling humiliated by her lack of control, BJ jumped up and grabbed her boots and gear, quickly putting them on.

Kody stepped back into the room just as BJ was fastening her utility belt. "I hope coffee and bagels are okay," she said, placing the tray down on the coffee table.

BJ glanced at Kody and felt her face flush when their eyes met; she quickly looked away. "It's um... fine. Thanks. But I really should get going."

Kody looked at BJ in confusion wondering what could have happened in the few minutes she was gone. BJ seemed very ill at ease and would barely meet her eyes. She had been perfectly fine when she went in the kitchen.

"Is something wrong? You didn't hurt yourself when you fell off the couch did you?" Kody felt suddenly contrite for laughing earlier. BJ could have been injured. She quickly stepped over to BJ and put her hand on her arm. She was shocked and hurt when BJ flinched at her touch.

"Please tell me what's wrong."

"Nothing... I've just... I've taken enough of your time," BJ said, finally meeting Kody's eyes. She had a swift flash of being held snuggly against Kody's chest; she flushed and quickly looked away. The worse part was she wanted Kody to wrap her in her arms again and never let go. *You are so pathetic!*

Kody wracked her brain trying to figure out what was going on, and then suddenly the light dawned. *She's embarrassed about breaking down last night.* The hardest thing last night had been leaving BJ sleeping on her couch. She had wanted so much to wake her up and take her to her bed and spend the night holding her tight. It wasn't about sex; it was about close emotional intimacy – something that had been sorely lacking in her life for far too many years. She too had opened herself emotionally to BJ last night and wasn't about to give that up.

Determined to set things right, Kody did what she had been wanting to do since she awakened that morning; she wrapped her arms around BJ and pulled her close.

"Thank you so much for last night. It meant a lot to me that you trusted me enough to let go."

BJ stiffened when Kody first wrapped her arms around her, but quickly relaxed into the embrace. She felt her eyes tear up at Kody's heartfelt words.

"I'm really sorry about losing it..."

"Don't! Please don't be sorry you shared that side of yourself with me." Kody pulled back and looked deep into BJ's eyes. "Don't hide yourself from me... Please."

The air seemed to crackle between them. Giving in to what had been building between them for the last few weeks, Kody leaned forward and pressed their lips together. The kiss was gentle, sweet, tender, and all the more arousing for it. She groaned, her arms tightening around BJ's back when her mouth opened to her. Kody delved into BJ's mouth, intent on exploring every millimeter. The world faded away and there was nothing but the feel of her tongue in BJ's mouth, the pressure of BJ's breasts against hers, the rapid beat of their hearts, and the surging of blood between her thighs as her hips began to rock.

Lack of air finally forced them apart. BJ clutched at Kody, burying her face against her neck. Her legs were shaking and she felt like her world had been turned upside down. She had never experienced anything like it in her life. She didn't think it was possible to come from a single kiss but Kody had damn near managed it. Finally regaining a bit of her composure she lifted up and met Kody's passion glazed eyes.

The kiss held a few surprises for Kody too. Besides the fact that she'd had the nerve to make the first move, which was amazing in itself, the kiss had been mind blowing. Her underwear was soaked with the evidence of the power of the kiss.

Her eyes locked on BJ's kiss swollen lips and her mind blanked. She had to taste those lips again. Just as their lips touched, a loud buzzing sound broke the moment.

"Sorry," BJ said as she reluctantly pulled away, her watch alarm blaring insistently. A quick look at her watch made her curse.

"What's wrong?" Kody was still in a bit of a fog with her thought process located somewhere between her legs.

"I have to go," BJ said. Leaving was the last thing on her mind. "I'm going to be late for work." She met Kody's eyes regretfully. "I really have to go."

Unwilling to break the closeness they had just shared, Kody reached out and gently grasp BJ's forearm before she could turn away. Not sure quite what to say she began to stammer, "We're um... okay... I mean um..."

BJ smiled shyly. "Yeah, we're good." Her head was still spinning with all that had happened.

"Are you going to be free later?"

"Sure. We have to follow up with the owners from the clinic last night. Once Neil and I take care of things at the office, we'll be by to get the information from you concerning the effected dogs."

Kody's shoulders slumped. That wasn't what she meant. She had hoped to see BJ on a personal level. Maybe she had read things wrong after all.

"Okay," Kody said, unable to hide her dejection.

You are such an idiot, BJ silently berated herself. Knowing that Kody had already taken a chance and put herself and her feelings out there, BJ knew it was time she too took a chance.

She reached out and tilted Kody's chin up until their eyes met. "What I would really like though is to get together after work. I want to be with you somewhere we can talk, and I can touch you." BJ gently stroked her thumb over Kody's cheek, smiling when Kody leaned into the caress.

Kody's expression immediately lightened. "It's a date."

BJ smiled brightly, and then groaned when her watch sounded again. There was no way she would have time to change before she had to be at work.

"I'm going to be late and so are you. See you later!" She couldn't resist planting on last quick kiss on Kody's lips before she rushed out the door.

Kody stood mesmerized, her lips still tingling from the too brief kiss. Thankfully, she didn't have to be at work until eleven a.m. Dr. Donaldson was working the early shift today. She couldn't help feeling vindicated by the fact that she had been right all along, although, in this case, she wished she had been wrong.

* * *

Neil dialed BJ's phone again with no success; he was really starting to get worried. She was never late. After he got home last night he had tried to phone her. He knew she had taken what had happened with the Shepard a lot harder than she should. He felt bad about it, but it was part of their job to keep the public safe. He had given up after several attempts and left a message with her voice mail. He hoped she'd gone out and had a drink and maybe gotten laid.

Just as Neil placed the phone back into the cradle BJ walked in the door. His eyes widened at the first sight of her. Her uniform was wrinkled and looked like she slept in it. Her short, spiky hair was standing up every which way. But most telling of all was the bright smile on her face and a sparkle in her eyes that he'd not seen before.

Neil chuckled; maybe she had gone out after all. "What happened to you?"

"Sorry, I overslept."

Neil snorted in disbelief. "I tried to call you last night and this morning. You didn't answer at your place or your cell."

BJ's hand went to her pocket where her cell phone was only to find it empty. She racked her brain trying to remember what she'd done with it. "Shit," she said, when she remembered. She had turned it off because the battery was low and set it on Kody's coffee table. Thoughts of Kody's coffee table quickly led to thoughts of Kody herself. A flash of memory of Kody's warm tongue invading her mouth caused a hot flush to course through her body. She quickly became lost in the memory.

"Earth to BJ." Oh yeah, this is going to be good.

BJ blushed. She could see the curiosity burning in Neil's eyes and unaccountably became tongue tied.

"I umm... my battery was almost dead. I turned it off." Before Neil could question her further she quickly made her way over to her locker and grabbed her extra uniform. "Just give me a couple of minutes and I'll be ready to go."

Neil laughed when his partner dashed out of the room. Something was definitely up and he was determined to find out what it was. BJ's behavior was so out of character; it just had to be because of a woman. His expression suddenly soured. The question was... what woman? Neil shook his head and laughed at the absurdity of it. *Na, no way it was Kody.*

* * *

Despite the seriousness of the situation at work, Kody couldn't seem to stop the bright smile that lit up her face. She had decided to come in a bit early to check on Rowdy and Willy, but even her concern for the two dogs couldn't dim her current happiness over the events earlier that morning.

"Good Morning," Kody said as she stepped into the clinic treatment area. The smile quickly dropped from Kody's face at the somber expression on her co-workers faces. "What's wrong?"

She glanced over at the cage Rowdy had been in the night before and was relieved to see the little beagle sleeping peacefully. When no one seemed willing to answer her, Kody immediately bolted for the back room that held the large kennels where Willy was. Her breath whooshed out in relief when she spotted the big dog. She knelt down by the kennel and softly called his name. Willy lifted his head and his tail thumped weakly.

"Hey big guy. How are you doing?" When the dog tried to stand, Kody quickly opened the kennel and stepped inside. "Easy, just relax. You're okay," she said while urging Willy to remain down.

As she stroked his big head, she glanced over toward the door to find Emily watching. Kody wondered what had happened that was so bad that the techs felt the need to send in Emily to tell her about it. With one last pat to Willy, Kody stood and stepped out of the kennel, closing the door behind her before turning to face the office manager.

Emily seemed uncharacteristically reluctant to meet Kody's eyes.

"Just tell me," Kody said.

Emily finally looked up and Kody was surprised by the mix of sorrow and anger that marred her features.

"Dr. Donaldson demands that you report to his office as soon as you arrive."

"What's going on?"

"Two Animal Control officers were here earlier this morning."

"Aw shit!" Kody hadn't thought they would show until she was here to give them the information and hopefully head off Dr. Donaldson.

Emily was momentarily shocked by Kody's outburst, then chuckled understandingly at the sentiment. "Yes, there's definitely been a lot of that hitting the fan this morning," she said drolly.

Kody couldn't help but laugh. It wasn't funny, but it was either that or cry. She had a very bad feeling she knew what was coming.

"What did he do?"

"Well he went on a rant of epic proportions, even for him, after they left. I don't know what he said to them but the two officers looked pretty angry when they left." Emily reached out and put a comforting hand on Kody's shoulder. That's when Kody realized her fears were justified.

"Tell me the rest."

Emily hesitated, reluctant to inform the young vet of the turn of events. Mentally squaring her shoulders, she knew Kody deserved to know what she was walking into.

"He said he was going to fire you as soon as you got here. He didn't want such an incompetent vet around his patients for another minute."

"This was in front of all the techs, I assume," Kody said.

"I'm so sorry, Dr. Garrett. We all know it's not true." Emily shuffled her feet and looked distraught. "I know we should all say something to him but..." her eyes filled with tears, "I'm sorry. I need this job and..."

"Hey, Emily, it's okay. I don't want any of you to say anything. I told Andrea that already."

"She told us," Emily said. "But it's just not right."

"I appreciate your support, but I don't want any of you to jeopardize your job."

Kody started in surprise when Emily closed the distance between them and hugged her tightly. Kody patted her back somewhat awkwardly. Emily just as quickly stepped away.

"I should get back to the front desk."

Kody nodded and followed Emily back into the main treatment room. Only one of the techs would meet her eyes. Kody was surprised; she expected to see a triumphant smirk on the woman's face. Instead Barbara's expression was one of deep anger when she met her gaze.

Anxious to get out of the uncomfortable atmosphere and resigned to her confrontation with Dr. Donaldson, Kody made her way down the hall toward his office.

CHAPTER 22

*F*OR A DAY that started out so wonderfully, this one had quickly gone down hill. First, they'd had a run-in with Kody's arrogant boss. It had never even occurred to BJ to call first and make sure Kody was at the clinic. She knew Kody worked on Tuesdays. By the time they managed to pry the necessary owner information from Dr. Blowhard she had developed a headache, not to mention the fact that she was concerned they had gotten Kody in trouble once again. Although, there was no way the clinic owner could claim that Animal Control had no justification in requesting patient information, he had tried. Things had only gotten worse as the day progressed. They had been forced to abandon the search of the effected dogs' yards when they got called to assist in the raid on a dog fighting ring that had turned out to be much larger and involve more animals than originally suspected.

It was already after five and they were just now heading back to the office. BJ was dirty, tired, hungry and heartsick at the condition of the dogs and puppies they had helped seize. Throughout the day, whenever she had a few minutes break, she had tried to call Kody. Repeated calls to her cell phone and home had gone unanswered.

Her worry had escalated to the point that she was willing to risk a call to the clinic. She waited impatiently for the phone at the clinic to be answered.

"Yes. Could I speak to Dr. Garrett, please?" BJ had already decided if asked she'd identify herself as a friend instead of an animal control officer. There was no sense getting Kody into any more trouble.

"What the hell are you talking about?" BJ said. "She worked there yesterday."

BJ listened for several seconds then snapped the phone shut, barely resisting the urge to smash it against the dashboard. If it had been hers she probably would have. Instead she tossed Neil's phone back to him.

"What the hell was that all about?" Neil asked.

"According to the clinic, Dr. Garrett no longer works there. They refused to give me any more information."

"What! Oh man, you don't think the bastard fired her cause of us being there this morning. He can't do that – can he?"

"No way in hell. Vets are required by law to report suspected animal abuse. Donaldson knows that, especially after this morning." They had threatened to file an obstruction charge against him before he finally admitted to having the effected dogs on the premises. "Kody didn't do anything wrong," BJ said.

Neil shrugged his shoulders. "Yeah, I agree, but what can we do about it?"

"We're going to go see Kody and find out what happened."

"Okay, we should be able to find some time tomorrow."

"No. Not tomorrow. Right now," BJ said. After the phone call to the clinic she had a bad feeling. Why wasn't Kody answering her phone?

"Come on, BJ," Neil said. "I'm tired and hungry. Can't it wait 'til tomorrow? Try to call her again."

"Fine, no problem. I'll just go over to Kody's place by myself." BJ didn't feel the least bit bad using Neil's interest in the vet to get what she wanted. She was worried and didn't want to wait to go back to base to get her vehicle before going to Kody's; it would take too long.

Neil quickly backpedaled. "No, no. You're right. We should make sure she's okay. Where does she live?"

* * *

BJ banged on Kody's door again. They had been at the front door for several minutes with no response from inside, except Blackjack's loud booming bark.

"Let's go. She's not here," Neil said for the second time.

"She's here. That's her truck."

Before Neil could protest further the front door was pulled open. BJ stared at Kody trying to figure out what was up. She had Blackjack by the collar with one hand and a glass of something in the other. It looked like Jack was the only thing keeping her upright. She was leaning heavily against the big dog's side.

"BJ... you came. Come in... Come in. Want a marjer... marriea... One of these?" she asked holding up the half full glass.

That's when BJ realized Kody was drunk. *What the hell!* Before BJ could react Kody let go of Blackjack and wrapped her arms around her neck. BJ struggled to keep both of them upright. Blackjack immediately rushed out the door toward Neil.

"He's friendly. Grab him," BJ said over her shoulder while she tried to hold up Kody and get the glass away from her at the same time. The last thing they needed was to have to chase Jack through the neighborhood.

Between the two of them they managed to get Kody and Blackjack safely back inside the house. BJ sat Kody on the couch, and then gave Neil a hand with Jack. She was relieved when the big dog listened to her and got in his bed.

"Hey, Neil, have a drink!" Kody said when she spotted him. "It's a party. I got fired," she said, laughing drunkenly.

Kody waved expansively and called to BJ, "Sit down... sit down," and promptly toppled over onto her side.

Neil sat down on the couch next to Kody and helped her to sit back up. He took the opportunity to wrap an arm around her to keep her upright.

BJ glared at Neil. He shrugged his shoulders innocently as if to say, "I'm just being helpful".

Kody looked up at BJ and blinked owlishly. "Oh... I'm being a bad hoster... hostsser... You need a drink."

BJ stepped forward at the same time Neil tightened his arm around Kody to keep her from getting up.

"That's okay. You've obviously had more than enough for all of us," BJ said.

Kody turned to Neil. "Nah. You'll have a drink with me, won't you?"

Neil grinned. "Sure. I'll have a drink with you."

"I like you, Neil," Kody said as she leaned close and patted his chest.

Neil smirked up at BJ and pulled Kody close to his chest. He knew he'd been right all along; the vet wasn't gay. "I like you too, Kody."

"Neil! She's drunk," BJ said. She moved to take up a seat on the other side of Kody.

"No, she's not. Lay off, BJ. She's just a little buzzed." Neil shifted position slightly on the couch drawing Kody closer.

Kody was oblivious to the tension between the two animal control officers. She patted Neil's chest again and began to ramble.

"Yeah, but you got the wong... wrong parts," Kody's voice drifted off as she lost her train of thought. She pushed herself away from Neil and looked up earnestly into his eyes. "You don't got the right parts... up here." Kody demonstrated by cupping her own breasts. And you got extra dangly parts down there," she slurred, pointing at his crotch. "I don't like dang... danly... those parts."

BJ couldn't help but laugh at the look of total outrage on Neil's face. Her laughter drew Kody's attention to her.

"See... she's got the parts right," Kody told Neil as she reached out and cupped BJ's breast, and then gave it a light squeeze.

BJ pulled back in shock. Her abrupt movement overbalanced an already unsteady Kody and she ended up face down in BJ's lap. BJ's face flushed a bright red as she peeled Kody's hand off her breast and then struggled to get her face out of her lap. Kody was being less than cooperative; she wrapped tightly around BJ's waist and didn't seem inclined to let go any time soon.

BJ shook her head in disbelief. She had been worried all day about Kody and the last thing she expected to find was the vet drunk as a skunk. Obviously, the whole story of what had transpired was going to have to wait. Kody was in no shape to tell them anything, other than what they already knew, that she had been fired.

BJ spared a glance at Neil to see how he was taking all this. He looked disappointed and a bit envious, however, he laughed when he caught BJ's eyes.

Neil wanted to be pissed at BJ, but it wasn't her fault he didn't have a chance in hell with the beautiful vet. Kody had made it quite clear, even in her current state that she wasn't interested in him, or any man for that matter. He'd tried to ignore it but he had sensed the attraction between the two women from the start he admitted to himself ruefully. Shaking his head at his partner's current predicament, he couldn't help the brief surge of envy.

BJ's brief inattention to Kody allowed her to move up and plant her face between her breasts. BJ fought back a groan as Kody began to rub her face against her breasts. She gasped outright when one of Kody's hands once again took possession of her breast.

"Well..." Neil said, "looks like you have everything well in hand. I guess I'll head back to the office."

"Come on, Neil. It's not funny. She doesn't know what she's doing. Help me."

Neil stared at BJ incredulously. Here his partner had a gorgeous woman throwing herself at her and she wanted her to stop.

"Neil!"

"All right. All right. But I still think you're an idiot," Neil said as he helped pry Kody away from BJ.

The drunken woman whimpered and tried repeatedly to wrap her arms around BJ. BJ finally managed to squirm out of Kody's grasp and off the couch. Kody looked up at BJ blearily as if nothing out of the ordinary had occurred.

"I need a drink," she said and reached for her half full glass.

BJ quickly grabbed the glass and pulled it away from Kody.

"I think you've had more than enough. It's time for all good little vets to go to bed."

A lecherous grin filled Kody's face. "Okay," she said eagerly, attempting to stand.

BJ managed to grab her before she fell. Kody somehow managed, even in her inebriated state, to wrap herself quickly around BJ like a second skin.

"Now what?" Neil said.

BJ glared at her partner. In any other situation, BJ would have loved to have Kody plastered against her, but she was drunk and there was no way she could take advantage of her, no matter what her rebellious body wanted. She had been wet and throbbing since Kody had unceremoniously landed face down in her lap.

"I can't leave her like this. Can you take the truck and my gear back to the office?" They had both removed their equipment belts and locked them in the truck before coming to the door. "I'm going to have to take a personal day tomorrow."

"What about your pickup?"

"Shit," BJ said, trying to decide what to do. She was having a hard time concentrating with Kody's hot breath blowing on her neck. "Just leave it in the lot. Once Kody sobers up tomorrow I'll get her to drive me over and pick it up."

"Okay, I'll let Diane know you're taking a personal day." Neil grinned when he realized Kody had started groping BJ's ass. He couldn't resist one last dig at his partner. "You two have fun now."

BJ growled at her laughing partner's retreating back. Once he was out of sight she reached back and pulled Kody's hand off her ass.

"Okay, Doc. Time for bed."

CHAPTER 23

*B*J STRETCHED trying to work the kinks out of her tight muscles. Sleeping on Kody's couch two nights in a row was taking a toll on her back. After she had gotten the inebriated vet into bed last night, she had borrowed a pair of sweats and taken a shower before raiding her kitchen for something to eat. After the ordeal Kody put her through she figured the vet wouldn't mind. Just the thought of Kody's drunken antics sent a heated flush through her body.

She had been too tired last night to clean up the mess of spilled margarita mix and tequila she found. She had gotten up this morning and taken care of Blackjack then set about cleaning up the kitchen and having a bit of breakfast. It was strange how at home and comfortable she felt at Kody's place. She looked down at Blackjack. The big dog had been following her around all morning and had plopped down at her feet while she had breakfast.

"Come on, big guy. Let's go wake up your mom." *Time for a little payback.*

BJ picked up a glass of juice and a bottle of aspirin; Kody was going to need them both.

* * *

Deciding even she wasn't that cruel, she left the Venetian blinds in Kody's room shut. After a third of a bottle of tequila BJ figured she was going to be in enough pain without any more help. Besides the light colored blind on the windows let in plenty of light. However, she didn't stop Blackjack when he approached the bed and poked at the blanket covered lump.

After several pokes, Kody shifted and tried to pull the blanket over her head. "Go away." That just encouraged Jack, who began to bark. Kody groaned pathetically. "Please... stop." One arm appeared out from under the covers and weakly tried to push the big dog away.

BJ decided she had suffered enough, for the moment at least. She quickly corralled Blackjack, and then turned back toward the bed to find a bleary eyed Kody blinking at her in apparent confusion.

"BJ?" Kody's head was pounding and her thoughts were muddled. She looked around confirming that she was in her own bedroom. She could not for the life of her figure out how she had gotten there, much less what BJ was doing in her room.

BJ sat down gingerly on the side of the bed. "How are you feeling?"

"Ugh... my head is killing me and my mouth feels like someone emptied a dirty ash tray in it. What happened?"

BJ chuckled causing Kody to wince and grab her head. "Here," BJ offered two aspirin tablets, "take these and drink a little juice."

Kody tried to lever herself into a sitting position to accept the offered items. That's when she became aware of her attire, or lack there of. She flopped back down with a groan and pulled the sheet up under her chin.

Her eyes were wide when they met BJ's. "Why am I naked?"

A bright blush instantly suffused BJ's face; she was sure the image of Kody's naked body sprawled out on the bed was forever seared into her mind.

"Oh God," Kody said.

BJ set the glass and pills on the nightstand, then scrubbed her hands across her face, trying to regain her composure.

"Oh, God," Kody said again as she immediately thought the worst. "Oh God...

"Will you stop saying that," BJ said, willing her blush to fade. She shook her head in exasperation; she wasn't the one who had something to be embarrassed about. She had just been trying to help.

Kody tried to compose herself as best she could. "What did I do?"

"What's the last thing you remember?"

Oh God, this is so not good. Kody closed her eyes and racked her fuddled brain, trying to remember. She clearly remembered the kiss she and BJ had shared...she was pretty sure that must have been yesterday. Then she went to work and... *Damn.* Kody's eyes popped open.

"I remember getting fired."

BJ nodded sympathetically. "Yeah, I know. I'm sorry. What about after that?"

Kody groaned. It was starting to come back. "Donaldson tossed me out of the clinic. Wouldn't even let me get my stuff. Said I had to come back when there were no clients there. "Kody squeezed her eyes shut trying to force her aching brain to cooperate. "I stopped by the store and picked up... some ice cream, I think. I came home and then... Oh God... the margaritas."

"Oh yes – the margaritas. Just how many did you have?"

Kody grimaced. "I'm not sure. I remember eating the ice cream, then I decided to rearrange the kitchen." Kody glared when BJ snickered. "I didn't just want to sit and mope. Anyway, that's when I found the tequila and margarita mix. Things are pretty fuzzy after that," Kody said sheepishly.

"I just bet they are," BJ said.

"It seemed like a good idea at the time," she said. Kody tried to bury her head in her pillow as BJ's gales of laughter assaulted her ears. "Stop, you're killing me."

BJ fought to get her laughter under control. She knew Kody was suffering, even if it was of her own making. "Tell you what, why don't you drink some juice and take the aspirin. A hot shower might help too. Once you feel a little better I'll try and fill in some of the missing blanks."

BJ stood up and turned to make her way out of the room. She wanted to give Kody some privacy – not to mention that seeing her naked body again and not being able to touch her would most likely kill her.

Kody still didn't know how BJ had ended up in her house, but she was grateful.

"BJ."

BJ turned back to face Kody. "Yeah."

"Thanks."

"No problem. I'll be in the kitchen when you're done. You should try to eat something."

* * *

"Well, you look a little better," BJ said when Kody shuffled into the kitchen with her hair still wet from her shower.

Blackjack jumped up and rushed toward his owner. BJ barely managed to grab his collar just in time. Kody didn't look too steady on her feet.

"It's okay. You can let him go."

Kody spent the next few minutes calming the big dog, no matter how bad it made her head hurt. It wasn't his fault she was an idiot, and she felt bad for neglecting him.

"I'm sorry, boy. You must be starving."

"Don't worry," BJ said. "I fed him."

Kody hung her head as her eyes filled with tears. BJ had not only taken care of her, but Jack as well. She couldn't remember the last time someone had done that.

BJ hurried to Kody's side. "Hey, it wasn't big deal. I just fed him. I hope you don't mind I got cleaned up and borrowed some clothes and made myself something to eat..." Unable to see Kody's expression she suddenly worried that she had over stepped her bounds.

Kody looked up with tear filled eyes. "It will take more than some borrowed clothes and a meal to repay you for everything you've done for Jack and me."

"I'm glad I could help," BJ said. "Come on, you'll feel better once you have something in your stomach." She was a bit uncomfortable with Kody's gratitude. It really was no big deal; she was more than happy to help.

BJ took her by the hand to lead her into the dining room. Kody looked longingly at the coffee maker.

"Coffee is the last thing you need," BJ said. "I've got some more juice and a dry bagel for you."

Kody allowed herself to be led to a seat at the table. She eyed the bagel and juice distastefully.

"Just a little coffee?" she said.

"Finish all that first, then we'll see how you're doing."

Kody shook her head stubbornly.

"You're dehydrated; coffee will just make it worse." At Kody's continued refusal BJ added, "I'm just trying to do what's best for you."

Kody's resistance immediately faded. "No fair," she said under her breath, just loud enough for BJ to hear.

BJ chuckled and pushed the glass of juice closer to Kody.

Finishing most of the juice and all of the bagel took all of Kody's concentration to guarantee they stayed in place. She finally pushed away her plate and met BJ's eyes. Not a word had been exchanged while she ate.

"All right. I'm not sure I want to know, but how exactly did you end up being here? Not that I don't appreciate it." Kody's brow furled as she struggled to remember. "That's the other thing... Was Neil here last night?" she asked sounding unsure.

BJ grinned. "Starting to come back to you, huh?"

"Just jumbled images. It doesn't make a lot of sense."

"Before I tell you what happened, maybe you could use that cup of coffee after all," BJ said.

"Oh God."

"Don't start that again. It's not THAT bad."

* * *

Kody almost spit out the sip of coffee she had just taken. BJ was in the process of recounting the previous evening's events.

"Dangly parts!" Kody had been mortified to learn that Neil had seen her drunk, but this was too much. "I did not say that!"

BJ laughed uproariously. "You most certainly did. Neil's poor little ego may never recover."

"Please tell me that's the worst of it."

BJ shook her head. "Sorry, wish I could."

Kody banged her head on the table and groaned in pain. "At least I wasn't naked." A horrifying thought suddenly struck. She lost what little color she had managed to regain. "I wasn't was I?"

BJ considered torturing her further, but one look at Kody's face and she relented. "Nope, that was after Neil left."

Although totally embarrassed, Kody felt a brief surge of relief. She could deal with BJ having seen her naked.

"Tell me the rest."

Kody buried her face in her hands as the story continued to unfold. She had never been so humiliated in her life.

BJ stopped after telling her about Neil leaving and how she managed to get her into the bedroom.

Kody forced herself to meet BJ's eyes despite the vivid blush on her face. "I am so sorry, BJ. There's no excuse for groping you like that."

BJ laughed. "Don't worry about it. I knew it was José talking."

"I will never drink tequila again," Kody said. "Please tell me I went quietly to bed."

"Would you like me to lie?" While it had been fun to torture her at first, seeing how contrite and embarrassed Kody was BJ was starting to feel sorry for her.

Kody seriously considered taking BJ up on her offer. Then she figured it was better to know the truth. *How bad can it be? She's still here... right.* Kody had a sudden flash of laying naked on her bed with BJ standing next to it looking down at her. *Oh God.*

"Tell me. I can take it." Another memory flashed, this time of BJ kneeling behind her and supporting her naked body. "I think," she added nervously.

BJ laughed and reached out to pat Kody's arm consolingly. It was readily apparent from the look on Kody's face that she was starting to remember more of what had transpired last night.

"I got you into your bedroom, and then realized you probably wouldn't be very comfortable sleeping in your chinos and an oxford shirt. So I helped you out of them." BJ wiggled her eyebrows. "You were very cooperative."

"Oh God," Kody said as another memory struck.

BJ shook her finger warningly at Kody. "Ah...ah. Let's not start that again."

"Sorry," Kody said. This was getting worse and worse.

"I had planned on leaving you in your bra and panties," BJ said. "I left you sitting on the side of the bed and went into the bathroom looking for a hamper to put your dirty clothes. By the time I got back to the bedroom, you'd taken off your bra and panties and were sprawled out naked on the bed."

BJ once again had a vision of the beautiful vet spread out in all her glory. When she finally managed to shake away the arousing image and meet Kody's eyes, they sported matching blushes.

"Before I could get you covered up, you mumbled something about the room spinning and tried to bolt for the bathroom."

As much as the sight of Kody naked haunted BJ, just as poignant was the feel of her bare flesh under her hands as she helped her to the bathroom, and then comforted her as she purged her system of the remaining tequila."

"Let me guess," Kody said. "I didn't make it by myself."

"Nope." Kody looked like she was praying the floor would just open up and swallow her. BJ tried to console the embarrassed woman. "But after I got you back to bed, you went right to sleep."

"Thank God for small favors," Kody said. She looked up barely able to meet BJ's eyes. "I don't even know where to begin to apologize. I can't believe I did something so stupid. I rarely have more than a couple of beers or a glass of wine at one time. I haven't been drunk since I was a freshman in college."

"Forget it. We all do things we regret sometimes. I'm just thankful I was here. I don't even want to think about what might have happened if you'd been alone."

BJ still vividly remembered an incident that happened during her senior year in high school. She had been out of town for the weekend and her best friend had decided to attend a party alone. They always went together and looked out for each other. Janice had gotten drunk, snuck back to her room and vomited while she was alone. She had aspirated and almost died. It was touch and go for several long weeks.

BJ was jerked out of her memories by the sound of Kody crying. She scooted her chair over next to Kody and wrapped her arms around her.

"Don't cry. Everything is going to be all right." Kody just cried harder. BJ urged her up and led her back to her bedroom. "Come on now. You're just tired. Everything will look better after you've had some sleep."

Kody wrapped her arms around BJ. "Don't go."

"I won't."

She pulled away from Kody, and then slipped under the light covers on the bed. Reaching out for Kody's hand, she pulled her into the bed with her. BJ smiled when Kody snuggled against her body. Allowing herself something she had wanted to do earlier, she slipped her fingers into Kody's silky curls and gently massaged her scalp. Kody sighed in contentment and quickly drifted off. BJ savored the feel of Kody in her arms before eventually falling asleep herself.

* * *

"Are you feeling any better?" BJ asked.

Kody nodded. She had woken a short time ago to find her head on BJ's chest and BJ's arms wrapped snugly around her. She was too comfortable and content to move.

"We should get up. You need to try and eat something more substantial than a bagel."

"Okay," Kody said, but made no attempt to move.

BJ knew they would have to get up eventually. She still needed to go get her truck and her rumbling stomach had awakened her almost a half an hour ago. However, she wasn't having much luck motivating herself to move. Nothing in her life had ever felt so right as holding Kody in her arms did. She was loath to break the warm sense of contentment currently surrounding them. As soon as they got out of this bed, reality was sure to rear its ugly head.

Reality intruded a few minutes later in the form of a poke in the side from a nose attached to a big hairy face.

BJ laughed quietly. "Looks like someone else is hungry too."

Kody smiled, loving the rumble of BJ's laughter under her ear. She lifted up enough to meet BJ's vivid green eyes. "Thanks for staying."

"Anytime."

Kody shook her head in amazement. "You are one special lady... you know that?" When BJ blushed and tried to look away, Kody put a hand on the side of her face and brought her head back up. "I mean it. You don't know how wonderful it makes me feel that you took such good care of Jack and me."

This time when their eyes met and held the room seemed to recede around them. Kody leaned down, drawn like a moth to a flame and pressed her lips to BJ's. The kiss was warm and as tender as Kody knew how to make it. It was a kiss of thanks and at the same time one of a promise of things to come.

They were both a bit glassy eyed when the kiss finally broke. They stared at each other, each hesitant to make the next move. Both unknowingly worried it was too soon, especially after everything that had happened.

Blackjack, never one to be ignored for long, ended the stalemate in his own unique way. In a single leap, he landed on the bed next to them and proceeded to try and lick them both to death.

"Jack, you big moose. Get down this minute," Kody said trying to escape the big slobbery tongue.

Jack nimbly jumped to the floor and woo woo'd his displeasure at being reprimanded.

"I can't believe he did that," Kody said. "He knows he's not allowed on the bed."

"Somebody's jealous," BJ said. She got up and went over to console the big baby.

Kody reluctantly followed BJ out of the bed. She was surprised to feel much better than she deserved to after her overindulgence yesterday. She still felt a bit achy and had a slight headache but nothing she couldn't live with. A glance at the clock provided the reason why; it was after six p.m. They had been asleep for six hours. With the sudden realization that it was now Wednesday evening for the first time something else occurred to Kody. She had been so caught up in thoughts of herself it hadn't dawned to her until now.

"Oh Damn."

"What's wrong," BJ asked in concern.

"I just realized you must have missed work to be here. Aren't you going to be in trouble?"

"Na. I took a personal day. Although, if you're feeling up to it I do need you to give me a ride to work so I can pick up my truck."

"Of course, I'm so sorry for all this, BJ."

"Will you stop that? I was happy to do it. I wouldn't be here if I didn't want to."

Kody immediately crossed the room to BJ's side. BJ smiled and readily opened her arms. Kody didn't need any other invitation; she eagerly snuggled into the warm embrace.

Blackjack's insistent prodding finally broke them apart.

Kody sighed dramatically. "Okay, okay. I get it. You're hungry."

BJ laughed reaching down to pat the big dog. "He's just like a big kid, isn't he?"

"Yeah, come on, let's feed the kid, then I'll take you out to eat before we go get your truck." Kody reached out and entwined her fingers with BJ's, needing this however small physical contact with her.

BJ grinned. She was happy to follow Kody where ever she wanted to go.

CHAPTER 24

"**W**OW, COFFEE and donuts. You must've had a good time."

BJ looked up to find a smirking Neil standing in the doorway of their office. She looked down somewhat ruefully at the donut in her hand. She had been looking over the reports from yesterday and hadn't been able to resist the smell of the freshly made donuts. As a rule, she rarely went for the overly sweet pastry that Neil preferred.

"What are you talking about?" BJ said.

"You must be trying to replace all those calories you burned off." Neil shook his head at the look of confusion on BJ's face. "You know, you and the doc – doing the wild thing."

BJ glared at her partner; he was so adolescent sometimes. "I told you. Nothing happened."

It had been hard to leave Kody last night. She had followed Kody back to her house after they picked up her truck. BJ had insisted on making sure she got home safely. Despite Kody's denials, she could see that the vet was still suffering from the aftereffects of the alcohol. They had shared an almost chaste kiss before BJ left. After spending two nights at Kody's it had seemed strange to return to her own apartment. What had always been a refuge from the world suddenly seemed empty and lonely without Kody. She had consoled herself with the fact that Kody had invited her to return after work today. To combat the unaccustomed feelings she had turned to the only thing she knew – work. She had called Neil to get an update on the poisoning cases.

"Lighten up, BJ. I was just joking." He still couldn't quite believe that BJ had actually taken a personal day. That had never happened in all the time they worked together. Neil walked over and peered into the bag sitting on his side of the desk next to a cup of coffee. He helped himself to one of the donuts. "Chocolate-filled, my favorite."

"I know. I bought them for you as a thank-you. I appreciate you following up with all the owners of the poisoned dogs by yourself yesterday."

Neil looked momentarily chagrined. "So what do you think?" he asked, nodding toward the reports in front of her.

BJ shook her head in disgust. "Like you said last night... We don't have shit. The same person must be doing this. Everything points to the fact that they're escalating. This is the longest string of poisonings yet. And according to Kody, they didn't use rat poison this time. She's not sure what they're using, only that it's deadly. If we don't come up with something soon, this bastard is going to strike again. There has to be some connection between all these cases. We're missing something, damn it!"

* * *

Kody checked out the clinic as BJ slowly drove by. It was almost eight o'clock and everyone should have been gone, but Kody wanted to make sure. They had been out at dinner and she had asked BJ to stop by the clinic so she could check on the dogs that had been poisoned on Monday. She might not officially work there, but was still worried about the dogs that had been poisoned.

"We need to go in the back," Kody said, directing BJ toward the back of the clinic.

The sight of the clinic cast a wave of sorrow over Kody's heart. She knew that she had done nothing wrong, but that didn't change the fact that she had been fired. It was going to be difficult to get another job. There was no way Donaldson was going to provide a recommendation; she would be lucky if he didn't badmouth her to any potential employer who called to confirm her previous employment.

BJ pulled her truck into the parking spot near the clinic that Kody indicated. She glanced at Kody and felt an instant rush of guilt at the expression on her face. Although Kody had denied it, BJ still felt she held some responsibility for Kody getting fired.

"I'm sorry."

Kody forced away the depressing thoughts and turned to BJ. Somehow she knew with one look at her face to what she was referring.

"I told you. It isn't your fault. My contract says he can let me go with thirty days notice without cause."

"But if we hadn't..."

Kody reached over and placed her fingers on BJ's lips forestalling any further protest. "No. If it hadn't been for this situation he would have found some other reason to get rid of me later. I'm just one in a long line of young vets Donaldson has used. He hires them on a two year contract like I have with a thirty day notice clause on either party's part – meaning I could leave with notice if I wanted. After completing two years, you become a partner and own 25% of the clinic. It's one of the reasons I was willing to accept the salary I did. But here's the kicker... If you work one day less than two years you get nothing. He finds an excuse to let everyone go sometime before their two years are completed."

"That bastard!" BJ said.

"Tell me about it. I didn't find out until I'd been here several months just how many vets had worked here before me. I'll give Donaldson credit, he talks a good talk. I believed him. I did ask the techs when I was here interviewing about the previous vet, but none of them said anything. Knowing what I do now about Donaldson I'm sure they were afraid of losing their jobs. Worst part of it is, by the time I figured it out I had really grown to like the techs, clients and the area. It's a great community and I liked feeling that I was helping the community where I live. Plus living only ten minutes from work is great. Even knowing what I did, I hoped that maybe this time it would be different." Kody shook her head in disgust at her naiveté. "I should have given notice and started looking for a new job as soon as I realized what he was up to."

BJ reached out and placed a consoling hand on Kody's arm. There was nothing she could say that would make this better.

"You sure you want to go in? You don't owe Donaldson anything."

"This isn't about him. Those dogs are my patients no matter what he says. I want to check on them and make sure there have been no other cases. You know he wouldn't call them in. We should check for new cases while I still have these." Kody held up her keys to the clinic. "If you'd rather stay out here, I understand." She was suddenly feeling a bit unsure about talking BJ into accompanying her to the clinic. Maybe that had been a mistake.

Giving Kody's arm one last squeeze, BJ smiled and reached for the door handle. "Let's go." Before she could open the truck door, the back door of the clinic swung open.

"Wait a second," Kody said. Her eyes widened when she saw the tech standing in the doorway with a black Labrador Retriever at his side. She quickly ducked out of sight; she knew the tech would not recognize BJ.

BJ watched the dark haired young man look around nervously, and then quickly close and lock the door to the clinic. Spooked by Kody's strange behavior, she ducked when he glanced over at her truck, although she didn't think he could see her in the dark. She lifted back up just in time to see him disappear around the corner of the building with the dog in tow.

"What the hell was that all about? Was that one of your techs?" BJ asked when she was sure he was gone.

Kody sat back up and peered out the truck window. "Yeah, that was Tom. He works part-time for the clinic. He comes in at night when we have an in-house patient that requires around the clock care."

"But why would he be taking a dog out of the clinic?"

"I have no idea. He shouldn't even have keys to the clinic. When he works he comes in before the tech on duty leaves and stays until a tech comes back in the morning to relieve him." Kody paled as a disturbing possibility occurred to her. "Oh no." She shook her head, refusing to believe it. "It can't be..."

BJ was worried by the look on Kody's face. "What? What's wrong?"

"I just remembered something. At the time it seemed strange but now..." Kody's voice trailed off as the scene played through her mind.

"Tell me."

"It was the Monday after you brought the pups over to my place and told me what you had uncovered about the poisonings. I decided to go into work early to catch up on my paperwork. When I pulled into the parking lot I saw Tom coming out the back door of the clinic. He didn't see me and was gone by the time I got out of my truck. I figured there must have been more poisoning cases come in over the weekend. I just couldn't figure out why he would be leaving before being relieved. The tech assigned to open the clinic arrived right after that. I mentioned it to her, but she didn't know anything about him being there. There hadn't been any new cases and Tom wasn't working. I don't know what he was doing in the clinic then either." Kody looked at BJ with a horrified expression. "You don't think he could possibly have anything to do with all this... do you?"

BJ's mind rapidly flipped through the possibilities. "How well do you know this guy?"

Kody sighed. "Not real well. He's only been working part-time for us for a few months. He seems like a good kid. He's always friendly and gave the impression that he really cared about the animals. I do know he works for other vet clinics in the same capacity. He works as a temp, just coming in when he's needed."

"Do you know what other clinics he works for?" BJ asked. Could this be the link they were looking for?

"I know of two others for sure. He works at a clinic in Pacific Beach and one in the South Bay."

Bingo! "Which just happen to be two of the areas that have had poisoning outbreaks," BJ said.

Kody looked heartsick. "I just can't believe he would do something like this. Even if he is the one doing this, what would he be doing in the clinic?"

"Maybe he didn't poison them, but it sure looks suspicious. I'm assuming there are a lot of drugs and chemicals around the clinic that with the right knowledge would be deadly to dogs.

Kody's face paled. "Oh – definitely."

"I think Neil and I need to pay this guy a visit tomorrow. Do you know his full name and where he lives?"

"His name is Tom Olsen. He lives a couple of streets over from me, on Madison. I happened to run into him awhile back in the grocery store and he told me he lived in the area. I don't know the address."

"Can you get his address from the clinic?"

Kody hesitated; she didn't feel right going into his personnel records. "I don't know..."

"It's better this way, Kody. If you don't give it to me then I'll have to go to the clinic and request it."

"But what if he's not –"

BJ quickly cut her off. "It's not worth taking the chance. What if he is? We'll just go talk to him; see what he has to say for himself."

Kody reluctantly nodded. "Okay, come on. Let me check on the dogs first then I'll get the information for you."

* * *

Kody paced her living room restlessly. BJ had dropped her off at home after they checked out the clinic. She had been relieved to find no further poisoning cases. Rowdy was still in the clinic but appeared to be very stable. He'd bayed loudly and begged for attention when she knelt down by his kennel. She had suffered a moment's panic when she went to check on Willy and found his kennel empty. A quick search produced his chart which included a note stating he had been released. While in the clinic she had quickly looked through the drugs and solutions that might have been used to poison the dogs, but couldn't find anything obviously missing. It had been pretty hopeless to start, in a vet clinic there was a diverse selection to choose from, any one of which, if used inappropriately could be deadly.

Everything had been going great. BJ had taken her hand as they made their way back to her front door; it had felt so right. When they reached the front door everything seemed to change. They had stared awkwardly at each other, neither seeming to know what to say. After several moments of uncomfortable silence they had said good night and shared a brief kiss. The only bright side of the moment was a promise to see each other the following evening.

She had wanted so badly to ask BJ to stay the night. It had been so wonderful to wake in BJ's arms, despite the circumstances. She wanted – no needed to experience that again. She had missed her last night. As she stood with her on the porch all her insecurities had overwhelmed her. Kody was afraid that BJ would get the wrong idea and see her as needy or worse yet, that she just wanted sex. Oh, there was no doubt, she wanted to make love with BJ, more than any woman she had ever known, but this was not about sex. It went much deeper than that and that in itself added to her fears. Even as her uncertainty made her hesitate, she had seen something in BJ's eyes that made her think that maybe... just maybe she had wanted to stay. Kody just hadn't been able to work up the courage to ask her for what she needed.

Kody flopped down on the couch in a fit of pique. "You are such a chicken shit." She jumped when the phone rang. A bright smile spread across her face; who else would be calling her this late except BJ. She grabbed it off the table not even bothering to check the caller ID.

"Hello."

"Dr. Garrett. This is Emily. I'm sorry to call you so late, but it's very important."

Kody felt a flush of guilt. Did the woman somehow know she had been in the clinic tonight?

"Um... How are you?"

"I've had better days," Emily said.

Kody could hear the stress in the office manager's voice. She might not work at the clinic anymore, but she did care about the staff with the obvious exception of Dr. Donaldson. She would gladly help if she could.

"What's wrong? Is there anything I can do to help?"

"As a matter of fact, you can. We need you to come back to work."

"What are you talking about Emily? Dr. Donaldson fired me."

"I know, but Dr. Donaldson isn't here. He hasn't been to work for two days."

"What?" Kody couldn't believe it; he never missed work.

"It's true. He didn't show up on Wednesday. I tried repeatedly to call him at home but there was no answer. He doesn't have a cell phone. Thankfully, there weren't a lot of appointments 'cause it was our half day. I really got worried when he didn't show up again today and I still couldn't get in touch with him. I contacted my nephew; he works for the Highway Patrol." Emily took a deep breath trying to keep herself under control. She still could not believe what happened. "Dr. Donaldson was in an auto accident Tuesday night; someone ran him off the road!"

Kody gasped. "Do they know that for sure?"

"Yes, the police were at the clinic early this morning. Dr. Donaldson is in Alvarado hospital; he's listed in critical condition."

"I'm sorry to hear that. I know we've had our differences, but I hope everything works out okay. As far as coming back to work, I can't do that. Dr. Donaldson fired me; only he can undo that.

"It's required by your contract that thirty days notice be given by either party. You haven't worked those thirty days yet," Emily argued.

"Dr. Donaldson waived the notice period. He owes me thirty days' pay. He chose not to have me work those days."

"Do you have that in writing?"

Kody felt her anger rise. "Whose side are you on, Emily? In case you don't remember, Dr. Donaldson humiliated me in front of the staff and threw me out of the clinic!"

"I'm on your side, Dr. Garrett. I hate what Dr. Donaldson did to you, but I'm also on the side of the animals. We have a responsibility to our patients." Emily sighed; she knew she wasn't handling this well. "Please, Dr. Garrett. We need you. I had to close the clinic yesterday and today and cancel all the appointments. If you won't work until Dr. Donaldson is able to tell me what he wants to do then I'll have no choice but to close the clinic until he recovers. The patients depend on us and to be perfectly frank, I need this job, and so do the rest of the staff. Please, come back to work, if only for thirty days."

Kody wanted to remain angry and say no after the way she had been treated, but knew she couldn't. She did feel a responsibility to the animals under her care. That was what had led her to sneak into the clinic tonight. Add to that the fact that animals were being poisoned and she had no choice. She had to be at the clinic to keep an eye on everything. Her conscience would let her do nothing else.

"All right, Emily. You win. I'll come back, but only for thirty days."

"Thank you so much, Dr. Garrett. Everyone will be so happy to have you back."

"I'll see you tomorrow, Emily. Good night."

Kody hung up the phone with a sigh. She was equal parts happy and frustrated to be going back to work. She was glad to be working but knew the likelihood of Donaldson being appreciative of her help was slim to none.

CHAPTER 25

$\mathcal{B}$J FILLED NEIL in that morning on the happenings of the night before, including the shocking phone call she had gotten from Kody after she got home. She didn't think the incident with Donaldson was in any way related to what was going on with the animal poisonings. Nevertheless, it had her worried.

BJ and Neil had canvassed the surrounding neighborhood where Tom Olsen lived, asking people about the poisonings, and then if they knew the vet tech. So far they had come up with zilch. With the exception of Tom's elderly landlady, no one they had found at home admitted to knowing the man. He lived upstairs in a small converted apartment on the third floor of the woman's Victorian home. She had nothing but high praise for the young man. After Mrs. Rusaitti had assured them that Tom was home, they had retreated to their vehicle to discuss a strategy for approaching the tech.

"I don't think we should tell him where we got our information," BJ said.

"Why not? It might spook him enough to get a reaction out of him. If it really is him, it's hardly like he's just going to confess."

"I know. I'm worried about the fact that he's escalating. None of the previous cases went beyond a few dogs baited with rat poison. There was never a second set of poisoning with an unknown agent that we know of. If he finds out that Kody was the one who told us about him, who knows what he might do."

"How do you want to handle it then?" Neil asked.

"I want this guy to know we're looking at him and that we know he's up to something. Maybe he's gotten cocky getting away with this for so long. Once we let him know we're onto him maybe it will spook him into stopping."

BJ did not hold out a lot of hope of that actually working. At this point, all they had was suspicion. That's what made this type of case so frustrating. The police had enough on their hands with human crime. It was a sad fact that animal abuse just wasn't a priority. Without someone seeing him, and being willing to testify or actually catching him in the act, their hands were effectively tied.

"All right, let's do this," Neil said.

* * *

Neil looked down at the shaggy haired, slightly built man, who answered the door. "Tom Olsen?" The man nodded reluctantly, refusing to meet Neil's eyes. He had a very unassuming appearance. Neil had a hard time picturing him as the type to poison dogs, but you never knew what someone was capable of just by looking at them. He still vividly remembered the case with the sweet, gray haired grandmother, who had invited them to have tea with her, and then calmly admitted to putting out bowls of antifreeze to poison the neighborhood cats because they were using her flower beds as a litter box.

"I'm Officer Martin and this is my partner, Officer Braden. We're with Animal Control. We'd like to ask you a few questions."

"What about?"

"Why don't we go inside and sit down," BJ said.

The man's eyes darted nervously up at Neil then over to BJ. "Okay." He turned and led them into the small apartment.

BJ looked around as they stepped into the living room. She didn't know what she had hoped to see, but there was nothing out of the ordinary in the room. There was one single room that encompassed the living room, a small kitchen table, and separated from the living room by a half wall, the kitchen.

Tom led them over to the small kitchen table. Neil could see the tight grip the man had on the back of one of the chairs. He sat down and BJ quickly followed suit. The tech stared down at the table for several moments before finally sitting down.

Neil stared at the tech, letting the silence stretch; silence could sometimes be a more powerful tool than any words.

"What... what did you want to talk to me about? I don't know anything," Tom said.

Neil worked to keep his expression stern. With his height and build he could be very intimidating when he wanted. *Works every time.* He could see the sweat starting to bead up on the younger man's upper lip.

"You don't know anything about what?" Neil asked.

Tom gulped realizing he had made a mistake. "I just meant that I don't know what I could possibly know about anything... that you might want."

"Where's your dog," BJ asked.

Tom's eyes darted fearfully over to BJ. "What dog? I don't have a dog."

"The one you were seen leaving the North Park Clinic with last night." BJ watched in satisfaction as the young man's face paled. *Gotcha.*

"Who told you that?" Tom looked ready to bolt his eyes darting nervously between the two officers.

"I don't know what you're talking about. I don't have a dog. I do work at North Park as well as two other clinics."

"So what were you doing in the North Park clinic last night?" BJ asked.

"I was working at the Pacific Beach Vet Hospital last night. You can check with them." Tom looked back and forth between the two officers. "What's this all about?"

"We're following up on the dog poisoning cases. You've taken care of some of those dogs, haven't you?" Neil asked.

"You think I had something to do with it?" Tom asked.

"Did you?" BJ said.

"No." Seeing the skeptical look on the two officers faces, Tom added, "You can look around if you want."

Damn it. "Sure, why don't you show me around," BJ said.

A quick tour of the small one bedroom apartment turned up nothing. No sign that a dog had ever been there. BJ had hoped to find something, anything to give them a clue that this guy was involved in the poisonings. She was realistic enough to admit it had been a pipe dream. The likelihood the tech would have something laying out that would incriminate him was close to nil. Even if they had found something, like cheese in the refrigerator and a box of rat poison under the sink, simply owning those items did not make you a dog killer.

After returning to the kitchen table, Tom seemed much more confident. She and Neil shared a frustrated look. They weren't going to get anything else out of him. This type of interview was a long shot at best.

"Thanks for your time," BJ said.

Neil turned back to the young vet tech when they reached the front door. "We'll be around, keeping an eye on things. Understand?"

Tom swallowed nervously and nodded. He watched the two officers until they reached their truck before going back inside.

* * *

"Dr. Garrett."

Kody looked up from the chart she was working on and smiled at Andrea. All the techs on duty had enthusiastically welcomed her back to the clinic. It had been a very long, tiring day. She had seen patients non-stop all day. Not only had there been all of today's patients to see, but also quite a few from Wednesday and Thursday that couldn't wait until Monday to be seen. They had finally seen the last patient a half an hour ago and everyone else had gone home. She was finishing up charts so she could finally go home as well.

"What's up?"

"There's a police detective out front asking to speak to you."

Kody's brow furrowed; she wondered what the police could possibly want with her. She rose and followed Andrea back toward the front.

Kody eyed the man waiting in the lobby. He was a short, stocky built man with blond crew cut hair. He looked nothing like she expected of a police detective. He could best be described as scruffy, looking like he could use a shave and a clean suit.

"I'm Dr. Garrett. What can I do for you?"

"Dr. Garrett," the man said, "Detective Marvin Swartz, San Diego Police Department. I'd like to ask you a few questions about Dr. Donaldson." He glanced over at Andrea. "In private."

Kody nodded and opened the half door that separated her from the lobby. "If you'll follow me, please. We can go into my office."

She stepped into her office, immediately regretting she hadn't taken the officer into Dr. Donaldson's office. Blackjack was stretched out on his blanket taking up most of the available floor space. At the sound of a gasp from the doorway, his head came up and he started to stand to face the stranger.

"Down," Kody said. She had heard the detective's reaction to the sight of Blackjack. She turned and perched on the edge of her desk, close to the dog. "He won't hurt you. He's friendly."

"I'm not afraid of a dog!" the detective said, angry that his tough facade had slipped so apparently. He stepped fully into the room. Despite his words he kept a wary eye on the big dog.

Kody fought to keep her expression neutral. She had seen this reaction to Blackjack before. "What can I do for you, Detective?"

"Where were you on Tuesday, between eight and nine p.m.?"

Kody's eyes widened as the significance of the time frame in question registered. "I was at home."

"Was anyone with you?"

"Yes, a friend. What is this all about, Detective? I thought you said you wanted to ask me about Dr. Donaldson. Not that I can tell you much."

"Can this 'friend' vouch for the fact that they were with you?" the detective said.

"Yes."

"What type of vehicle do you drive, Dr. Garrett?"

Kody was starting to get irritated. "I'm not answering any more of your questions 'til you tell me what this is all about."

"I'm asking the questions here." Swartz glared at Kody, taking an intimidating step toward her. He quickly took a large step backward at the threatening rumble emanating from the huge dog at the vet's feet.

"Quiet, Blackjack," Kody said. His head sunk back down to the blanket at his owner's reprimand.

Swartz glared at the big dog with false bravado before once again turning his attention to Kody.

"I'm investigating the hit and run involving Dr. Donaldson."

"And you think I had something to do with it?" Kody asked.

"It's my understanding that he fired you on Tuesday, yet here it is Friday and you're back at work..." The detective let the sentence hang; his insinuation was clear.

Kody stared at the detective in disbelief. He couldn't possibly believe that she had anything to do with what happened to Dr. Donaldson, but obviously he did.

"I'm required by my contract to work for thirty days after being given notice of termination."

"So why haven't you been here since Tuesday?"

Where the hell is this guy getting his information?! "Dr. Donaldson verbally waived the notice period. The office manager asked me to come back and work so that the clinic would not have to be closed while Dr. Donaldson recovered."

"Pretty convenient for you... Wouldn't you say? He's out of the way and you're back at work."

Kody felt her temper rise. This was ridiculous; she had had enough of this jerk. "Are you charging me with something, Detective? If you are, I want to have a lawyer present for any further questions."

"I'm just trying to do my job, Dr. Garrett."

"I understand that, however, I don't appreciate your insinuations. If you have a specific question to ask me – ask it."

"What type of vehicle do you drive?"

"A Ford Explorer."

"What color is it?"

"Dark blue." Kody met the detective's eyes challengingly. "Why?"

Swartz held her gaze for several moments before deciding to answer. "A dark colored SUV was seen forcing Dr. Donaldson's car off the road. Is your Explorer here?" Kody nodded. "I'd like to take a look at it," he said, staring hard at her.

Kody tried hard to reign in her temper. She knew she had done nothing wrong, but it was never a good idea to piss off a cop. This was serious business. "My truck's out back. You're welcome to look at it."

She led the way out to the back parking lot. Kody watched impassively as the detective looked over every inch of her truck.

"Okay?" Kody asked when the detective returned to her side.

"I appreciate your cooperation. If I need anything else I'll let you know." With that the detective turned and walked away.

Kody stared after him for several moments before heading back to the clinic.

CHAPTER 26

𝒦ODY'S DOUBTS began to assail her as soon as she hung up the phone. Maybe she shouldn't have called her; it was late and BJ had worked all day too. They had talked earlier in the day. Kody had called to see how the interview with Tom had gone and to cancel their dinner date. She had felt bad at the time, but knew with the workload it would be late by the time she got home. They had made plans to get together the next day, after Kody got off work. She figured that would work out well since she only worked a half day on Saturday. Kody wasn't even sure now how she had ended up calling BJ. She had stewed all the way home after her run-in with the detective at the clinic. Having gotten herself so worked up on the way home, she had walked into the house and before she realized it was talking to BJ. Just the sound of her concern had made Kody feel better.

On hearing what had happened, BJ had insisted on coming over. Kody had halfheartedly protested. Now she was feeling guilty about it; she should have refused. No doubt BJ was tired after a long day at work. Maybe she should call her back and tell her not to bother coming over. Kody lost track of time as she vacillated over what to do. She started when the doorbell rang and Blackjack ran for the door barking excitedly. Kody hurried after him.

"Hey," Kody said, smiling at the sight of BJ. Right or wrong she wanted her here she admitted to herself reluctantly. She grabbed Blackjack's collar and pulled him away from the door. "Come on in."

BJ followed Kody into the living room. "How are you holding up?" She couldn't believe the police could suspect Kody of having anything to do with Donaldson's accident. Hearing the strain in Kody's voice as she recounted her questioning by the detective had brought her protective instincts out in full force. She wished she had been there to give the abrasive officer a piece of her mind.

Kody shrugged, her back to BJ. "Okay, I guess... I'm sorry if I sounded like a big baby on the phone."

BJ sat the bags in her hand down on the coffee table and approached Kody. She reached out and turned the other woman to face her. Seeing the look on her face, BJ didn't hesitate and immediately stepped forward and wrapped her arms around Kody.

"You have every right to be upset."

Kody sighed as her head came to rest on BJ's shoulder. The tensions of the evening started to slip away. She couldn't explain it but everything seemed to looked better from the circle of BJ's arms. "He was just doing his job."

"I know. The guy didn't need to be such an asshole about it. He could've contacted you at home instead of work."

"I'm sorry I dragged you over here; you must be tired."

BJ placed a soft kiss on Kody's forehead. "I want to be here for you."

Kody lifted her head and their eyes met. She saw nothing but honesty and compassion in BJ's emerald gaze. "I want you here."

Whatever it was between them surged to life. Neither was aware of moving, but the next moment their lips met in a warm gentle kiss. One of them, or it might have been both moaned as their bodies cleaved together. The world faded around them. There was nothing but the rapid beating of their hearts, the pounding pulse echoing between their thighs. As one their passion rose, their tongues dueling in an increasingly erotic dance.

They were brought back to earth by an insistent nose poking between them. Kody growled in frustration as the kiss broke; she was panting with arousal. She glared down at Blackjack's innocent face. She wanted to be mad at the big dog but just couldn't. It wasn't his fault that he wasn't used to sharing her attention. Still wrapped in BJ's arms she spared a quick glance at her, hoping she wasn't angry at the dog for interrupting them. Her fears were quickly put to rest.

"It's a good thing I really like you," BJ told the dog. "Otherwise..."

Blackjack poked BJ in the side and woofed, letting her know just what he thought of that.

BJ laughed and spun Kody around so that she was between her and Blackjack. "Ha! Can't get me now," BJ said. He woofed and tried to dodge around his owner to reach BJ. She quickly shifted keeping Kody between herself and the rambunctious Dane.

Blackjack barked loudly in frustration. He prodded Kody in the back several times as he tried to reach BJ.

Kody laughed enjoying the game. Finally she called a halt; she was starting to get dizzy.

"All right, you two. Enough. I'm not a play toy."

BJ grinned. "Ah... come on. You can be my toy. I promise to play nice with you."

Kody felt a rapid flush cover her face as her mind flashed back to her laying face down in BJ's lap with her hand on BJ's breast. She buried her face in BJ's neck in embarrassment.

BJ reached with one hand to pat a still bouncing Jack trying to calm him down, but never let go of her hold on Kody.

"Oh... what was that blush all about?" BJ whispered in her ear, "Tell me."

BJ's hot breath blowing in her ear caused a shiver to trace down Kody's spine. She looked up at BJ and saw the grin on her face, and her eyes sparkling mischievously.

Kody's brain abruptly disengaged from her mouth. Her eyes locked on BJ's breasts. "I was just remembering already playing with your toys."

BJ's body reacted instantly to Kody's words and heated gaze. She vividly remembered the feel of Kody's hands on her. Her body flushed at the memory.

Kody grimaced appalled at what had just come out of her mouth. "Oh God, I'm sorry. That was totally inappropriate," she said and dropped her arms from around BJ.

BJ came out of her lust induced stupor when Kody tried to pull away. She tightened her arms around Kody. "Don't be sorry. I'm not."

"But I... I groped you and –"

BJ placed her finger on Kody's lips. "And I enjoyed every minute of it," she said.

"You did?" When her memory returned that was the thing that had bothered Kody the most about that night. Although she knew they were attracted to each other, well attracted was a bit of an understatement, but still, she felt as if she had forced her attentions on BJ.

BJ laughed. "You have no idea! Remember I told you I took a shower after I got you to bed?" Kody nodded. "Well, I didn't use any of your hot water."

Kody's eyes widened, and then a huge grin nearly split her face. "Yeah?"

"Oh yeah," BJ said.

Blackjack decided he had been ignored long enough. A loud woo woo caused both women to jump.

"What?" Kody asked with a mock glare at the big dog.

Now that he finally had his owner's attention, Jack trotted over to the bags BJ had left on the table and prodded one of them with his nose before turning back to look at Kody pleadingly.

Kody had been so caught up in her own thoughts when BJ arrived she had not even noticed the bags.

"Oh! Zippy burgers. I love those." She pulled away from BJ and quickly hurried over to the bag.

"Well, I can see where I rate around here," BJ said.

Kody looked up guiltily with a French fry half way in her mouth. "Sorry," she said, then quickly swallowed the fry. "I only had time for a granola bar at lunch and I didn't get any dinner. I'm starving."

BJ laughed good-naturedly. "I figured. That's why I brought them for you."

Kody was momentarily chagrined at her behavior. She stepped back over to BJ and placed a quick salty kiss on her lips. "Thank you."

"You're welcome. Let's eat."

* * *

BJ watched in satisfaction as Kody finished off her second burger, and then chased the last bit of French fry on her plate. She was pleased that her offering had been so heartily accepted.

Kody leaned her head back against the couch with a contented sigh and closed her eyes.

"Feeling better?" BJ asked.

Kody turned toward her companion and opened her eyes. They were shaded to blue with her contentment. "Much better. Thank you so much for doing this." Kody glanced over at Blackjack who lay sound asleep on his bed. "I know Blackjack appreciated his burger too." Kody chuckled and shook her head. "I can't believe you brought him his own burger. Now he's going to expect that every time."

BJ laughed. "Ah, come on... He's a growing boy." She was suddenly overwhelmed by a huge yawn. "Sorry about that."

"I should be the one apologizing, you shouldn't..."

BJ slid over to the couch cushion next to Kody. "None of that now. I told you earlier. I came because I wanted to be with you." BJ fought to stifle another yawn. For some reason she had not slept very well the last two nights.

Kody glanced at the clock and groaned. It was much later than she realized, almost midnight. As much as she didn't want BJ to leave she needed to get some sleep if she was going to be functional at work tomorrow. She met BJ's eyes regretfully.

"I guess I should let you go. Unfortunately, I have to be at work bright and early tomorrow."

"What time to you think you'll be done? We're still on for lunch... Right?"

Kody smiled brightly. "If everything goes well I should be done by twelve thirty. I'm looking forward to going to Western Steak Burger. I've driven by there quite a few times, but never stopped to try it."

"It's a great place. You're going to love it."

"You sure you don't want me to meet you there?"

"Na. You just call me when you're done at work and I'll come by here and pick you up," BJ said.

Kody tried frantically to think of something else to ask. They had made the arrangements on the phone earlier. She knew she was just trying to delay the inevitable of BJ's leaving. She was taken by surprise by a big yawn.

BJ reluctantly rose to her feet, followed by Kody. "Well I guess I should go."

Kody trailed BJ to the front door. She struggled with what she needed and what her pride would allow her to ask for. Kody still remembered well the sting of Jocelyn, her one and only girlfriend, harping on how needy and clinging she was. Although it had turned out Jocelyn's complaints were more to keep Kody from questioning where she spent her time when they were apart, the comments still affected Kody even after all these years.

As had happened the previous night, they stared at each other awkwardly when they reached the front door.

BJ had no interest in returning to her lonely apartment, but couldn't figure out how to ask Kody if she could stay without giving her the wrong impression. While the kiss they had shared earlier had been electric, this wasn't about sex. She wanted to stay and spend the night with her arms wrapped around Kody. It had been a long, stressful week for both of them.

BJ struggled with what to say. "Been a long week, huh?" she said.

"Has it only been a week? Sure seems much longer." Kody's eyes brimmed with tears as she thought of the events of the week. "I can't believe everything that's happened..."

BJ immediately engulfed Kody in a warm hug. "I know. It's been a tough week for both of us, but you especially." BJ tightened her arms around Kody drawing her closer to her body. "Everything will work out. I just know it."

Kody snuggled into BJ's warm embrace. Savoring the warmth of the other woman's body, and drawing strength from her unflagging support, Kody found the courage to ask for what she so desperately wanted.

She pulled back enough to meet BJ's eyes. "Would you stay here with me tonight? I –"

"Okay," BJ said, not giving Kody a chance to say anything further.

"You will?" BJ nodded. A sweet smile of pleasure spread across Kody's face. She reached out and grasped BJ's hand. "Come on then, let's go to bed." Kody had taken a single step toward her bedroom when she realized how that sounded. She turned back to BJ with a worried look on her face. "I umm... I mean umm... to sleep... Not that I don't... I just... ." Kody's head dropped toward her chest in embarrassment as she struggled to explain herself.

BJ reached out and placed her fingers under Kody's chin gently urging her head up. She smiled when their eyes met. "I understand. I just want to hold you tonight – nothing more."

Kody felt a wave of relief sweep over her. She wrapped her arms around BJ and gave her a quick squeeze. "Thank you," she whispered in her ear. She immediately pulled away and once again took BJ's hand to lead her into her bedroom.

* * *

Kody had been so relieved and happy that BJ had agreed to stay she had forgotten about Blackjack. After lending BJ a pair of sleep pants and a tee shirt, she had gone to take care of Jack while BJ got ready for bed. As she headed back toward the bedroom, Kody was struck with a sudden attack of anxiety. Although she wanted BJ to stay, and they had already shared a bed, she was unaccountably nervous. She peeked into the bedroom before entering, relaxing a bit when she realized BJ was still in the bathroom. Quickly grabbing sleepwear for herself, she headed for the guest bathroom.

BJ stepped out of the bathroom surprised to find Kody still missing. She stepped out into the hall to look for her and noticed the light leaking from under the door of the bathroom off the hall. BJ wandered back into the bedroom and stood next to the bed. She didn't feel comfortable getting into the bed without Kody. The hair on the back of her neck prickled and she turned to find Kody standing in the door way watching her.

BJ's smiled as Kody made her way toward her. "Scooby Doo... huh. Why am I not surprised?" BJ asked. She laughed outright when she got a closer look at the sleep pants. Not only were they covered with images of Scooby Doo and large dog bones, but small banners as well. "Bad to the bone?"

Kody laughed good-naturedly. "Look who's talking."

BJ glanced down at the pants she was wearing. They were bright blue and covered with Superman's emblem. "But they're yours too, so it doesn't count. Now if we were at my place..."

"What do you sleep in?" Kody asked innocently.

BJ waggled her eyebrows. "Wouldn't you like to know? Maybe I sleep in the buff."

The tee shirt BJ was wearing was a bit snug on her across the shoulders and chest. Her breasts were outlined beneath the shirt. Her assets were stimulating enough seen through the shirt. Just the thought of BJ in the nude was enough to make Kody's eyes momentarily glaze over. Her erotic fantasy was interrupted by a large yawn.

BJ chuckled and reached out for Kody. "Come on, Doc. Let's get some sleep."

Kody climbed into the bed, all her nervousness from earlier was gone. She moved toward BJ as soon as she got into the bed. Kody smiled when BJ offered her shoulder without hesitation. She rested her head on her shoulder and snuggled against her side. Nothing had ever felt this right in her life. She lifted up enough to reach over BJ and flipped her alarm to the on position before turning out the bedside light. She sighed audibly as she snuggled back down and BJ's arm tightened around her back.

"Good night," Kody said into the dark.

BJ placed a gentle kiss on Kody's forehead. "Sleep tight." BJ lay awake for a while after Kody's breath evened out and it was clear she was asleep. When she came over tonight she never expected to find herself in Kody's bed again. She couldn't remember the last time she had spent the night in a woman's bed, much less one she hadn't had sex with. While she wanted very much to make love to Kody, for now she was more than content to hold her and enjoy the feel of her warm body next to hers. Before she realized it, she too drifted off to sleep.

CHAPTER 27

WAKING UP in BJ's arms had been heavenly. It had been surprisingly natural and hadn't felt the least bit uncomfortable. Despite Kody's protests, BJ had insisted on getting up with her. They had shared a quick breakfast before she was forced to leave for work. She had been inordinately pleased that she had been able to convince BJ to stay and relax before heading home. There had been no reason for her to leave for home at seven thirty in the morning. Blackjack had seemed a bit confused when she got ready to leave, but had been perfectly happy to stay with BJ. Kody hoped she had a quiet, quick day at work.

She could not keep a huge smile off her face as she approached the back door of the clinic; she felt great. Nothing could ruin her mood today. That assertion was put to the test when she stepped into the treatment room of the clinic to find Barbara working on supplies.

Barbara looked up when she heard the door swing open. "Good Morning, Dr. Garret," she said.

Kody was a bit taken aback by the tech's smile and friendly tone. She still remembered the woman's angry stare on the day she was forced to leave the clinic after being fired.

"Good Morning, Barbara." Kody quickly turned to business. Only two techs worked on Saturday, due to the normally light patient load. "What do we have on today?"

"It's a pretty quiet day – mostly routine follow-up appointments."

"Please let me know when the first patient arrives. I'll be in my office."

At Barbara's nod of acknowledgement, Kody turned and made her way toward her office.

* * *

The morning had gone quickly, with no surprises just as Kody had hoped. She was back in her office going over patient charts. The last client of the day had cancelled, so she was using the time to finish up her charts. As soon as noon rolled around she was out of here. Kody couldn't wait to get home.

The sudden niggling sensation of being watched caused her to turn in her chair. Barbara was standing in her doorway with the strangest expression on her face.

"What's up?" Kody asked. She had been pleased with Barbara's work today. The tech had been polite, helpful and professional. Kody was relieved that her problems with the tech were over.

Barbara smiled brightly at Kody as she moved to stand next to her desk.

Kody felt an immediate urge to stand but resisted the impulse. "What can I do for you?"

Barbara placed a warm hand on Kody's shoulder. "I just wanted to let you know how glad I am you're back."

Kody pulled away from the woman's touch and stood up. She once again damned her small office. Even without Blackjack here there was just no room to maneuver.

"Thank you, but it's only for a short time," Kody said.

A momentary grimace appeared on the tech's face and her voice hardened. "It was terrible what Dr. Donaldson did to you. You deserve to be the one here running the clinic, not him."

"Dr. Donaldson owns this clinic and you work for him. I'm sure he'll be back to work soon." Kody had no idea if that was true or not but was becoming uncomfortable with the direction the conversation was heading.

Barbara shrugged negligently. "It'll be great working together." She smiled at Kody, and then her eyes momentarily dropped to Kody's chest before looking back into her eyes. "I know this great place in Hillcrest. You're going to love it; the food's fantastic. I'll be ready to go as soon as I close up."

Kody's mouth dropped open in shock. *What the hell!* She took a step backward onto Blackjack's bed trying to put some distance between herself and Barbara. So much for thinking the woman had finally gotten a clue.

"Listen, Barbara I –"

"Dr. Garrett."

Kody glanced toward the door in relief. She slipped past Barbara and quickly urged Lisa out into the hall. She didn't see the lethal glare Barbara sent Lisa's way.

"What can I do for you?" Kody asked subtly leading the tech away from her office. Maybe Barbara would take the hint and go back to work.

"Mr. Alton is here to pick up Rowdy. He'd like to talk to you."

"No problem. Put him in Room One. I'll go get Rowdy and be right there."

* * *

Things had gone well with Rowdy; he had passed his release physical with flying colors. The self-inflicted bite wounds were healing very well. So far he didn't seem to be suffering any after effects as a consequence of being poisoned. Kody just wished she knew with what he had been poisoned. She couldn't help worrying about possible long-term effects. Mr. Alton had been thrilled to have his buddy back.

Kody peeked out the door of the exam room. Seeing the coast was clear she headed for her office. She cautiously looked in the door before entering. *This is ludicrous. I shouldn't have to sneak around the clinic.* Kody pushed her office door shut before flopping in her chair. "Only twenty-eight more days to go," she said.

She quickly finished up Rowdy's chart before gathering her belongings. Kody headed for the front of the clinic knowing Lisa was working the front desk. It was after twelve o'clock so her duties were done. She wasn't about to stick around and chance being stuck in the clinic alone with Barbara.

Lisa was in the process of shutting down the computer system at the front desk.

"See you on Monday," Kody said as she headed for the front door. Her quick exit was stymied when the door refused to open.

"Hang on," Lisa said. She pulled the keys out of her smock pocket and moved to open the door for Kody.

Just as the lock clicked open, Kody heard her name being called. She glanced up to see Barbara approaching from the hall with a determined look on her face. She turned her back and with a hasty thank you to Lisa quickly slipped out of the clinic. Kody heard her name yelled angrily as she neared the corner of the building. She never looked back and hurried around the corner to the parking lot behind the clinic.

CHAPTER 28

$\mathcal{B}$J HUMMED in time to the radio as she finished preparations for Kody's surprise. The ringing phone interrupted. A glance at the caller ID screen caused a grin to break out on her face as she picked up the phone.

"Hey," BJ said. "All done?"

"Yeah. I just got home and couldn't help noticing –"

"It's not my fault," BJ said.

Kody chuckled. "Sure. He just got in your truck by himself."

Kody had panicked when she arrived home and realized Blackjack was missing. She breathed a sigh of relief when she found BJ's note, and then shook her head in exasperation. She couldn't believe that BJ had gotten suckered into taking the big dog with her. Although Kody knew she drove a Toyota Tundra Xtracab, she had a hard tonneau cover on the back instead of a cap. That meant the only way she could have taken Blackjack with her was to put him in the cab. That must have been a sight.

"Almost," BJ said. At Kody's disbelieving laugh, she hurried to explain. "I was all set to leave. I let him out to take care of business. When he came back in everything was fine 'til I picked up my keys. He ran to the front door, his tail wagging a mile a minute and started woo wooing. That's when I told him he couldn't go with me..." BJ's voice turned accusing. "You could have warned me!"

Kody couldn't help but laugh; she was easily able to picture the scene.

"It's not funny. It was horrible. His tail went down between his legs and his whole body slumped... and then... he began to whimper and shiver. I just couldn't leave him like that; it was awful."

Having fallen victim to Blackjack's manipulations, Kody easily sympathized with BJ's predicament – although, she did find it very humorous. It was nice to know she wasn't the only one affected by

Blackjack's theatrics. She was convinced he practiced that face and act in the mirror when she wasn't home.

"So how is Mr. Pathetic now?"

BJ glanced over to where Blackjack lay. He was stretched out on his side, easily covering the length of her couch with his head on the armrest, sound asleep. She knew it was a good thing Kody couldn't see him or they would both be in big trouble. She didn't allow Blackjack on the furniture, but BJ hadn't had the heart to reprimand the big dog when he crashed on her couch.

"He's fine. Sound asleep as we speak."

"What did you two do? Sounds like you wore him out."

"Just ran some errands," BJ said. She didn't want to ruin the surprise. "You ready to go to lunch?"

Kody felt a brief flash of worry remembering Barbara's anger at her quick departure from the clinic. The woman had followed her once before, the first time she met with BJ and Neil. She had looked around on her way home but not seen any sign of her.

"Kody?"

"Oh, sorry. Yeah, lunch sounds good."

"What's wrong?" BJ heard a change in Kody's voice.

Kody shook away her concerns. She would not let Barbara or anyone else ruin her time with BJ.

"It's nothing. I'll be waiting for you and Jack."

BJ wasn't convinced but didn't push the issue. "See you in a few."

* * *

Kody linked her hands behind her head and stretched on the blanket where she lay. She couldn't have asked for a better afternoon. It was a picture-perfect southern California day. The storm from earlier in the week had finally blown itself out. The sun was shining in a brilliant blue sky, normally only seen on a postcard, especially in early March. There was not a cloud in sight and the temperature was in the upper seventies.

Instead of going to the restaurant as planned, BJ had surprised her with a picnic in Balboa Park. They had started with a tour of the park's extensive rose garden, and then driven to a secluded section of the park for a late lunch. The area adjacent to the picnic grounds was busy with people using the nearby tennis courts and pool. The tiny picnic area itself, sheltered within a grove of eucalyptus trees was deserted, even on this beautiful Saturday afternoon.

Kody smiled at her companion when she moved to lie down beside her. "This was a wonderful surprise. The roses were just beautiful and lunch was fantastic. Thank you for doing all this." Kody arched her back and signed in contentment as she stared up at the sky, just visible through the trees. "This was just what I needed. I can't remember the last time I went on a picnic."

BJ's eyes were drawn to Kody's breasts as she stretched. The tee shirt she was wearing stretched taut. BJ felt her own nipples tighten.

Not getting a response, Kody glanced over at BJ and smirked when she noticed where her eyes were glued.

"BJ... My eyes are a bit higher than that."

BJ met Kody's eyes and grinned unrepentantly. "I'm glad you had a good time. I figured we both needed a break from everything that's been going on."

Kody's eyes dimmed as she once again was reminded of the situation with Barbara.

BJ moved closer and turned on her side to face Kody. She lifted up, so she could look down into Kody's eyes. "What is it? I know something is bothering you. I could hear it in your voice earlier. Did something happen at work?"

Kody hesitated. Not because she didn't want to tell BJ, but because she didn't want to ruin their day. She met BJ's gaze and saw the worry and concern in her eyes.

"It's noth –"

BJ reached out and placed a gentle finger on Kody's lips. "It's something if it's bothering you. Please trust me."

"I do," Kody said. She reached out and linked her fingers with BJ's bringing them to rest on her stomach. Kody proceeded to fill BJ in on all that had gone on at the clinic with Barbara including the tech's attempt at blackmail. As her story concluded with her most recent run-in with the tech, Kody could see the anger on BJ's face and almost feel it radiating from her body.

"That bitch. She's the little blond that gave me such a hard time?"

"Yes. She's the one. That's why I was a bit nervous about going out today. Since she followed me before..."

BJ immediately glanced around the park making sure no one was near. They were the only people in the picnic area. She turned her attention back to Kody. Taking a chance, she decided this was the perfect opportunity to discuss with Kody something she had wanted to talk to her about ever since she found out she had gotten fired.

"Have you ever considered coming to work for Animal Control?"

Kody was nonplussed at the rapid change in subject. "No. Not really."

BJ smiled at her confusion. "We're always looking for good vets. You need to get away from that clinic. Between the situation with Donaldson and now Barbara..."

"I know. Emily asked me yesterday if I would stay on. Dr. Donaldson won't be coming back anytime soon. He's in pretty bad shape. According to Emily, there's a chance he might lose part of his leg."

"What did you tell her?" BJ asked. She felt bad for the vet. Despite the fact that he was a jerk, no one deserved to be hurt like he had. Still, she would feel better to have Kody away from there completely.

"I told her I'd have to think about it. Donaldson did fire me. What's to keep him from eventually coming back and claiming I tried to steal his business? I just don't trust him. At least I'll get paid while he's gone; Emily is the one who writes out the checks. Emily insisted that as office manager she has the authority to hire and fire, but I'm not sure that applies to another veterinarian. She wants to hire me back so that I can stay past the thirty days, but she admitted she has only hired the vet technicians." Kody ran a hand through her hair in frustration. "I just don't know what the hell to do. I don't feel right just walking away knowing everyone else will lose their jobs. Plus with this poisoning thing still going on..."

BJ understood Kody's frustration; there were no easy answers. Her main concern at this point was the vet tech bothering Kody. "Do you want me to have a talk with Barbara? I'd be more than happy to tell the little bitch to back off and that I don't appreciate her messing with my girlfriend."

Kody grinned wondering if BJ realized what she had just said.

"What?" BJ said, confused by Kody's reaction.

Kody reached up and slipped her hand behind BJ's neck and pulled her down. Just before their lips met she whispered, "Girlfriend. I like that."

BJ groaned into the kiss as her body made contact with Kody's. She opened her mouth willingly to the welcome invasion of Kody's tongue. Forgetting where they were, the kiss quickly flamed out of control. BJ moved on top of Kody. She shifted her weight and pressed her thigh between Kody's legs, her own hips jerking at the contact.

They were brought back to their senses by a loud warning growl from Blackjack. BJ immediately moved off Kody. Her heart was pounding frantically in her chest matched only by the pulsing between her legs. She looked at Kody wide-eyed, stunned that she could lose control so easily.

BJ sat up and scrubbed her hands over her face. She looked around trying to spot what had made Blackjack react. She was shocked by the big dog's sudden growl. He had been stretched out sleeping peacefully on a blanket next to them. After the rose garden, she and Kody had romped with him, throwing a toy back and forth to run off some of his excess energy. He had conked out after getting his share of their lunch.

Not seeing anyone near, she turned her attention back to Kody. She had moved over by Blackjack and was petting the upset dog; he was still looking around suspiciously. BJ felt a flash of anxiety that Kody was angry at what had just happened between them. After all, they were in a public place. She moved over and took up a place on the other side of Blackjack.

Reaching out, she placed her hand gently on Kody's back. Relief washed over her when Kody turned to face her and smiled.

"I'm really sorry about that," BJ said.

"Don't be. I'm not." Kody leaned over Blackjack and brushed her lips lightly against BJ's before pulling back to smile into her eyes. Blackjack growled threateningly making them both jump.

Kody looked down at the dog, ready to reprimand him. She assumed he was jealous, but his attention was not on her or BJ. He was looking off toward the trees furthest away from them that delineated the rim of a canyon.

"Knock it off, Blackjack."

BJ noticed where his attention was as well. "Maybe I better go see what's over there."

Kody put her hand on BJ's arm to stop her from getting up. "It's probably just a squirrel or maybe a coyote wandered up from the canyon." Kody's mind was on things other than wildlife. Just the brief press of BJ's thigh between her legs had her long-suffering libido screaming. She ran her hand up and down BJ's arm leaving goose bumps in her wake. "Why don't we just go home?"

BJ swallowed heavily and her arousal soared anew at the look of promise on Kody's face.

"Yeah. Let's get out of here."

As they gathered their belongings, Blackjack continued to growl low in his throat despite his owner's reprimand. He was trying his best to warn them, but only he seemed to be aware of the malevolent presence lurking nearby.

CHAPTER 29

*B*J LEANED against the kitchen counter watching as Blackjack devoured his dinner. She wasn't quite sure what had happened. They had both been quiet on the ride back from the park. BJ's mind had been filled with images of what might happen when they got back to Kody's. She had been sure she had read an invitation in Kody's eyes at the park but now she wasn't as confident. She was beginning to think she might have misread the situation. The silence between them was beginning to grow slightly awkward.

Kody puttered around the kitchen getting down wine glasses and opening a bottle of wine. She had every intention of taking up where they left off at the park; it was all she could think about on the way home. She had been struck by a sudden case of nerves as soon as they stepped back into the house. It had been a very long time since she had been with anyone. She had no idea what BJ liked. What if she couldn't please her? Kody was also worried about how she looked. She kept meaning to lose that extra fifteen pounds but never seemed to get around to it. What if BJ was turned off by her less than perfect figure?

She was drawn out of her reprieve by a cold nose poking her. She grabbed a drool towel off the counter and wiped Jack's slimy drool covered face. "That's a good boy. Go on now." She patted the big dog and sent him out of the kitchen.

Kody picked up both glasses of wine and walked over to hand one to BJ. Their fingers brushed as she took the glass and Kody shivered. Kody looked deep into BJ's eyes and the air crackled between them.

Oh, the hell with it! This is ridiculous. Kody set her glass down and reached out for BJ's before she could even take a sip. She took BJ's face between both her hands and placed a searing kiss on her lips.

They were both panting by the time the kiss broke. Kody brushed her lips against BJ's again just barely making contact. "Please tell me you want this as much as I do?" Kody whispered against BJ's lips.

"More," BJ said before bringing their lips together once again. She wrapped her arms around Kody, and then pressed her back against the counter. She licked Kody's bottom lip, urging her to open to her. She moaned into the kiss as her tongue swept into Kody's mouth intent on mapping every inch.

When the kiss finally broke for lack of air, BJ's body was soaring. She could feel her desire soaking her underwear. She brought her hands up to palm Kody's breasts as she placed wet, open mouth kisses down her neck.

Kody's arms wrapped around BJ's back and pulled her closer. They still had their clothes on and she could already feel the first warning tingle of orgasm. Not wanting things to end so quickly she pulled back.

"Wait," Kody said, trying to regain control of herself. *God, what this woman did to her.* "Wait."

BJ struggled for control. She forced her hands to be still and met Kody's eyes; she nearly lost herself in the vivid depths. Fighting her raging arousal she finally managed to ask, "What's the matter?"

"If we don't stop... I'm going to come."

BJ groaned; she was very close herself. "And that would be bad – why?"

Kody's eyes bore into BJ's. "Because I want to feel your naked skin on mine when I come."

"Oh God," BJ said feeling her knees weaken and threaten to give out. Kody's eyes had gone impossibly darker with her declaration. They were the most incredible shade of blue she had ever seen. "Bed. Now."

Kody nodded incapable of speech. She grabbed BJ's hand and led her down the hall to her bedroom. Blackjack jumped up from his bed to follow. Kody motioned BJ into the room and blocked the door to keep the big dog out. "Go get in your bed." With that she unceremoniously shut the door in his face.

Kody moved over to the side of the bed where BJ stood waiting. The walk down the hall had allowed the flames that had threatened to consume her in the kitchen to calm to a simmer. They stood by the side of the bed and kissed for several long moments. Still feeling just the tiniest bit insecure, Kody stopped BJ when she tried to tug her shirt out of her pants. "You have me at a distinct disadvantage here." She laughed at BJ's confused look. "You've already seen me naked."

"But you've already felt me up," BJ said.

"And you returned the favor in the kitchen. Very well I might add."

BJ smirked. She reached down and pulled her tee shirt from her jeans and without another word pulled it over her head. She grinned at Kody's raised eyebrow. The sports bra came next. She stood nude from the waist up before Kody silently encouraging her to look her fill.

Kody's playfulness vanished at the sight of BJ's naked torso. The flash of arousal the view inspired was almost painful. BJ's breasts were medium size with light brown nipples already tight with arousal.

"Your turn," BJ said.

Kody's fingers trembled as she reached out for her shirt to bare herself to BJ. She locked eyes with BJ only breaking contact to pull the shirt over her head. She quickly removed her bra and watched as BJ's eyes dropped to her chest.

Her breasts were larger than BJ's their weight causing them to hang slightly on her chest. Her nipples were taut, almost painful. She resisted the urge to use her hands to cover the slight love handles at her waist.

BJ forced her eyes up to meet Kody's. She was surprised to see what looked like trepidation in her gaze.

BJ took a step closer, their bodies not quite touching. "You are beautiful."

Kody blushed prettily at the compliment. She reached out tentatively and gently palmed BJ's breast. She groaned at the feel of the hard nipple pressing into her palm.

BJ pressed forward bringing their bodies together and trapping Kody's hand between them. She whimpered at the feel of their bare breasts pressing together. Her arousal was quickly reaching a fevered pitch. She slipped a hand between them and tried to open Kody's belt.

Kody felt BJ fumbling with her belt and pushed her hands away. She stepped back unable to bear another second of the restricting clothes. She pulled open her pants and pushed them and her underwear down. She was momentarily stymied by her shoes but quickly kicked them off, and then pulled her socks off.

BJ swiftly followed suit, struggling to bare her flesh. Her arousal made her fingers clumsy. When she finally managed to fight her way out of her clothes she looked up to find Kody watching her hungrily. BJ felt another bolt of arousal and was afraid she would come on the spot.

In the blink of an eye, she closed the distance between them, using her body to push Kody back toward the bed. They landed with a soft thump and a loud groan from both of them as their bare bodies made full contact, BJ urgently pressed her thigh between Kody's legs. Her hips jerked at the feel of Kody's hot, slick flesh against her leg. She shifted bringing her own sex into contact with Kody's warm thigh.

Unable to stop herself, she began to thrust against Kody. She lost the final thread of her control when Kody's hands slid down her back and grasped her ass pulling her close as she began to thrust back. The world dimmed down to the exquisite point of pleasure between her legs as the pressure rapidly built. Perspiration coated them both liberally, causing their bodies to slide together in the growing conflagration. BJ felt Kody tighten under her and cry out. It set off the fire coiled in her belly and it spread through her body consuming her.

* * *

BJ's eyes slowly fluttered open as she became aware again; she wasn't sure how much time had passed. Her head was resting on Kody's chest and she was half covering her body. She could feel the rapid beating of Kody's heart.

BJ lifted her head to meet warm, slightly glazed looking blue eyes. She moved off Kody to lie on her side next to her. She ran her fingertips up and down Kody's stomach in gentle strokes, watching as goose bumps appeared in the wake of her touch. "What just happened?"

Kody was still a bit dazed. She had never experienced such a powerful release. "I think I had an out of body experience."

"You too, huh?" BJ said. Her hand slid up and gently stroked Kody's breast while running her thumb over the turgid nipple. When Kody sighed loudly in pleasure, she leaned down to lave the nipple with her tongue. "Want to try that again?"

Kody's only answer was a hand on the back of BJ's head pressing her closer to her breast.

BJ's explosive climax had relieved some of the pressure of her earlier frantic arousal. She wasn't sure if the powerful orgasm had been a fluke caused by several years of abstinence or the natural culmination of her incredible attraction to Kody. She looked forward to enjoying a leisurely exploration of Kody's body to find out.

Kody whimpered when BJ abandoned her nipple and moved back up to kiss her. The whimper turned to a moan as BJ's tongue plunged into her mouth and her hand took up worship of the neglected breast. When the kiss finally broke, Kody's acute arousal had returned with a vengeance. She could not remember ever being this aroused with either of her two previous lovers. She was frantic with the need for BJ to touch her where she needed her most. She pressed a hand on BJ's shoulder urging her lower.

BJ moved down planting open mouth kisses along Kody's neck and across her upper chest. Her hand stroked Kody's breasts before sliding down the plane of her abdomen. She stopped when her fingers encountered the dark, curly hair between Kody's legs. Kody's legs spread in invitation; her hips already beginning to move. BJ groaned as her own arousal burned in her belly. She struggled to keep herself under control.

BJ took a nipple in her mouth and began to suckle as her fingers slipped into the wet, hot heat waiting for her between Kody's thighs. She wanted so badly to be inside Kody, to fill her, and for a few precious moments, to claim her completely.

Kody's head thrashed back and forth on the pillow; her moans filled the air. "Please... Please..."

BJ released the nipple in her mouth reluctantly. "You want me inside?" she whispered in Kody's ear. She pressed just the tip of her finger against Kody's entrance. It took all of her remaining self-control not to plunge deep. "Do you... Do you want me inside you?"

Kody was beyond speech. She reached down covering BJ's hand trying to push her inside.

"Say it," BJ said.

"Yes... Yes... Inside."

BJ pressed home, groaning as the hot, tight walls surrounded her finger. Kody's back arched and she cried out, her body trying to draw BJ deeper.

"More," Kody said.

BJ pulled out enough to add a second finger, and then began to thrust, her palm sliding against Kody's clitoris with each downward stroke. Her hips began to move in rhythm with Kody's. She pressed against Kody's side seeking relief for the building pressure between her own legs even as she continued to plunge deep inside her.

BJ tore her eyes away from the sight of her fingers disappearing into Kody's depths when she felt the muscles around her fingers start to flutter. She wanted to see Kody's face when she climaxed. Kody's inner walls clamped shut on BJ's fingers locking her in place as her body arched as if electrified; her climax roared through her body. It was the most amazing thing BJ had ever seen. BJ jerked against Kody's hip; her own orgasm taking her by surprise. Her eyes closed as the pleasure spiraled down her legs.

* * *

BJ's eyes slowly blinked open. Her head was once again resting on Kody's breast. *Wow! That first time wasn't a fluke.* She could still feel slight aftershocks pulsing around her fingers. She lifted up her head to find Kody's eyes still closed. As she moved up to kiss Kody her fingers shifted inside of her causing a loud moan to escape Kody's lips. BJ grinned, placing a soft kiss on her lover's slack lips.

"Hey... You okay?"

Kody forced her eyes open. "It was that out of body thing again," she said.

"I'm going to pull out now," BJ said.

"Kay." Kody's internal muscles clenched as BJ withdrew from her depths. She groaned her eyes snapping shut as her body reacted.

BJ cupped Kody's sex protectively. "Okay?"

Hearing the worry in her voice Kody opened her eyes. She smiled lovingly at BJ. "Never better. That was amazing... Both times."

BJ grinned happily and snuggled against the warmth of Kody's body, laying her head back on her chest. She sighed in contentment when Kody began to run her fingers up the back of her neck and into her short hair, murmuring in pleasure at the feel of the silky strands against her fingertips.

Before either realized it they had both drifted off, wrapped in the warmth of each other's arms.

* * *

Kody stirred a bit disoriented by the unaccustomed weight pressing her down. Her brow furrowed unsure what had awakened her. A bright, contented smile appeared as the memory of their love making flooded her. She opened her eyes and looked down at BJ sleeping contently with her head on her chest. She couldn't resist running her fingers through her cropped hair. Kody had thought the short, clipper cut hair would be harsh, but it was soft and silky to the touch. She placed a soft kiss on the top of BJ's head when she murmured in her sleep and pressed closer.

Kody started at the sound of something hitting her bedroom door. A high pitched whine was quickly followed by a thump. Guilt immediately flooded her. *Blackjack.* She had forgotten all about him. She cautiously began to ease away from BJ, not wanting to wake her.

BJ grumbled in protest at losing her warm pillow. She tightened her grip on Kody. "Where are you going?" she said.

"I need to let Blackjack out."

BJ reluctantly opened her eyes becoming aware of the insistent whining coming from outside the bedroom.

"Damn. I forgot all about him," BJ said. She sat up in the bed the sheet pooling at her waist.

Kody slipped out of the bed, and then leaned back down for a quick kiss. Her hand reached out of its own accord and gently caressed a breast in passing. "Go back to sleep."

BJ groaned and grabbed Kody's hand pressing it back to her breast. Now that she was awake, all of her was starting to wake up. "Come back to bed."

Kody was tempted. A loud thump against the door reminded her why she was getting up in the first place. She forced herself away from BJ and grabbed a pair of sweat pants and a tee shirt out of a nearby drawer. "I'll be back as soon as I take care of him."

BJ watched Kody hurry from the room. "Dogs! They're as bad as kids," she said. It didn't take long for her to start to feel bad. It wasn't Blackjack's fault he had to go out. It wasn't like he had a choice and could let himself out. Not to mention the fact that she was on his turf and he wasn't used to having to vie for his owner's attention.

A quick glance at the clock showed it was still early, barely six am. She wasn't sure what time they had come into the bedroom last night. Now completely awake, her bladder made its presence known. Getting out of bed, she opened the same dresser drawer she had seen Kody take her clothes from. She found another pair of sweat pants and a tee shirt; she figured Kody wouldn't mind. It wasn't the first time she had borrowed her clothes. After taking care of business, she went in search of her missing lover.

* * *

BJ smiled as she watched Kody lavish attention on Blackjack as he ate. It showed what a loving, caring woman she was. She felt her arousal grow as memories of the previous night filled her head. Now that she knew what delights lurked beneath Kody's clothes she realized she was going to have a hell of a time keeping her hands to herself. Then again, maybe it wouldn't be a problem. If Kody's earlier response to her touch was any indication, she would welcome her.

Becoming aware of being watched, Kody looked up to find BJ watching her with a hungry look on her face. Kody was pretty sure food wasn't what she was hungry for. She absently wiped Blackjack's face and gave him a fond pat, never taking her eyes off BJ.

"Go on, Jack. Go play," Kody urged the big dog, her thoughts already elsewhere.

Kody wasn't quite sure how it happened but the next thing she knew she had BJ pinned against the refrigerator and was kissing her senseless. She slipped her hands under the tee shirt BJ was wearing and caressed her bare breasts. Kody groaned the sensation of BJ's firm breasts in her palms fueled her arousal. She had barely touched BJ earlier and was determined to remedy that right now. Overwhelmed by an overpowering need to taste her, Kody broke the torrid kiss and dropped to her knees.

BJ's eyes widened when Kody suddenly jerked her pants down; her legs spread without conscious thought. Her head slammed back against the refrigerator as Kody's tongue delved between her folds. BJ moaned, her mind going blank as Kody began to feast. She yelped when Kody's warm tongue was suddenly joined by something big and cold between her legs. Her eyes flew open and she glared at Blackjack. He wagged his tail at her totally clueless; he just wanted to join whatever game they were playing.

"Go away, Blackjack," Kody said trying to push the big dog away. She had been so lost in the smell and taste of BJ she had not been aware of his return to the kitchen.

BJ yelped again when Blackjack poked a very sensitive spot. She tried to help Kody hold him off while she grabbed her pants.

"I'm sorry, baby," Kody said, helping BJ pull her pants up. She glared at Blackjack. Reaching out she grabbed BJ by the hand and pulled her toward the bedroom.

Blackjack followed them down the hall. When they reached the bedroom door, BJ urged Kody inside, and then turned to growl at Jack. BJ smiled in satisfaction when the big dog flinched. She unrepentantly slammed the door in his face.

CHAPTER 30

*B*J HUMMED to the radio in her truck as she made her way home. She was tired, tender, and incredibly content. She and Kody had spent most of the day in bed, finally being driven out by hunger and dehydration. They had taken care of Blackjack, shared a quick sandwich, drank a half gallon of orange juice between them and ended up right back in bed. It had been wonderful and exhilarating; BJ felt like she could walk on air. Kody was an incredible lover, not to mention being the most responsive woman she had ever known.

BJ shivered, her body flushing with memories. The second time they had come out of the bedroom a disgruntled Blackjack was awaiting them on the other side of the door demanding some attention. Sated for the moment, they ordered Chinese food for dinner. While they waited, they had gone out into Kody's small backyard and given Jack some much needed play time. Things had degenerated during dinner. It started out innocently enough; she had offered Kody a shrimp from her fingers. It quickly went down hill from there and they ended up frantically pulling each others clothes off, food forgotten. Blackjack attempting to join in had sent them running for the bedroom once again.

It was late by the time they emerged, after nine p.m.; both were totally spent. They had hydrated themselves, neither willing to get far from the other. As they were getting ready to go back to bed — to sleep this time, reality intruded when BJ remembered tomorrow was a workday for both of them. Not wanting to have to leave extra early in the morning BJ decided to head home to pick up clean clothes and her uniform. She smiled at just the thought of returning to Kody's arms.

BJ grimaced when the truck behind her suddenly turned on their bright lights. She looked in the rear view mirror and her eyes widened when the vehicle pulled up almost on her bumper. She took her foot off the gas and slowed down trying to get the driver to back off.

BJ gasped her hands tightening on the wheel when the vehicle behind hit her bumper. She tried to see who it was, but due to the bright lights she couldn't see the driver. All she knew for sure was the vehicle was some type of SUV. She pulled into the right lane in an attempt to get away from the nut in the truck. She pulled her cell phone off her belt and flipped it open. She had her thumb on the speed dial button for 911 when she saw movement off to her left. BJ breathed a sigh of relief that the truck was going to pass her.

It was not to be. When the truck came even with her pickup the driver slammed into the side of her vehicle. She pushed the button on her phone instinctively, and then grabbed the wheel with both hands trying to bring the truck under control. She swerved off onto the shoulder of the freeway before managing to jerk the truck back onto the road.

BJ looked over at the other truck just as they passed under a street light. Her eyes widened in recognition as her gaze locked for just a moment with the driver. The dark vehicle pulled away, and then slammed into her truck again forcing her off the road. BJ fought for control, but it was a losing battle. Her truck slid into the ice plant along the freeway, and then bounced down the embankment. The truck came to a sudden stop when it reached the bottom; the impact was jarring. Her airbag deployed, but BJ was no longer aware of what was happening. She had struck her head on the side window on the way down.

* * *

Kody whistled as she washed dishes. She figured she better get as many chores done as she could before BJ returned. Kody was tired, very sore, and couldn't be happier, although, she didn't think she could have another orgasm if her life depended on it. It probably hadn't been a particularly good idea to try and make up for six years of celibacy in one day, but she didn't regret a second of it. BJ was incredible and had taken her to heights she never knew were possible. Kody had always laughed at the mind blowing orgasms couples in romance novels always seemed to experience. She had snorted in disbelief, assuming it was poetic license on the part of authors to make the book more exciting. She silently offered apologies to all the authors she had doubted. It was not only possible, but even more incredible than they described. Kody's mind floated off, reliving some of the most stimulating memories. By the time she came back to her task the water had turned lukewarm. She smiled, draining the water and refilling the sink to wash the last two glasses. As she was putting the last glass on the draining board the doorbell rang. Kody glanced at the clock and grinned. Her lover had been gone less than an hour; BJ must have made record time going home and coming back.

Kody dried her hands and quickly headed for the front door. She heard Blackjack's booming bark from the patio, but decided to leave him out there until she had a chance to greet BJ.

"Hey, babe," Kody said as she pulled open the door. "Welcome ba..." Kody's mouth dropped open in shock; this was not happening. "What are you doing here?"

CHAPTER 31

KODY STARED at the person on her porch incredulously. "What are you doing here," she repeated.

"Aren't you going to invite me in?" Kody's unexpected guest asked with a friendly smile.

Kody's thoughts were whirling; this was just too surreal. She looked past her visitor in hopes of seeing BJ's truck pull up.

Kody flinched; her attention snapping back to her smiling visitor when a hand landed on her arm and squeezed.

"Let me in."

Kody jerked her arm away from the unwanted touch. "If you don't leave right now, I'm going to call the police," Kody said.

In a split second the intruder's expression turned ugly. "I don't think so." Kody gasped, stumbling back as a large Buck knife was waved in her face. "That's more like it," the intruder said, slipping into the house and shutting the door before Kody could react.

Kody was speechless as she was grabbed, and then roughly shoved into the living room. At the sight of the interloper, Blackjack pushed his nose against the patio door handle and began to growl. Kody winced and stumbled over the corner of the coffee table when the point of the knife pricked her lower back.

"Sit down."

Kody sank down onto the couch. She was shaking inside, her anger having given way to fear. She prayed that BJ got delayed and didn't walk in on this. She looked up at the blond with the knife.

"What do you want, Barbara?"

"Oh, now you're interested in what I want," Barbara said. She began to pace rapidly back and forth, her voice growing in volume. "It's too late now. You ruined everything. I helped you. I got you your job back and how did you repay me? You betrayed me with that glorified dog catcher. She's a whore!"

Barbara moved swiftly toward Kody and flipped the coffee table over. Kody cowered back against the sofa as Barbara loomed over her with the knife. "Did you think I wouldn't find out? I saw that bitch on top of you in the park. Did she fuck you – Did she?"

Sensing his owner was in danger, Blackjack began to bark frantically and jump against the patio door.

"Shut that mutt up or I will."

Kody's mind was reeling with Barbara's revelation. She didn't want to take her eyes off Barbara, but didn't have much choice. Kody leaned over the armrest of the couch so Blackjack could see her. She was so scared it took two tries to get her voice to work.

"Quiet, Blackjack. Be quiet. That's enough," Kody said as firmly as she could. She could hear the quaver in her voice; she silently begged the dog to listen to her. Blackjack stopped barking, but continued to stand at the glass door watching. Kody looked back up at Barbara. The woman was obviously a sociopath and Kody was beginning to wonder if she was going to get out of this in one piece.

Barbara glanced over at Blackjack, and then back down at Kody. A smile appeared on her face; it was chilling. She looked over at the dog again.

Kody cringed, a shiver chasing down her spine when Barbara began to laugh. It was not a good sound. Barbara looked down at her, her eyes gleaming with a fevered light.

"Perfect. Perfect," Barbara said to herself. She picked up a small backpack she had dropped next to the couch. "Over there," she ordered Kody with a wave of the knife, pointing toward the dining room.

Kody slowly stood up. She glanced down at Barbara once she had regained her feet. She had a good half a foot in height on the woman and at least forty pounds. She glanced around surreptitiously for something she could use as a weapon.

Barbara pushed Kody roughly toward the dining room table the knife pressed against her lower back. "Don't even think about it," she said, as if she knew exactly what Kody was contemplating.

As they neared the door, Blackjack began to growl, his lips pulled back as he snarled fiercely at the woman threatening his owner. Barbara ignored the dog. She put the backpack on the table and calmly opened it.

Barbara took several cellophane wrapped items out of her pack. Kody's brow furrowed. The woman took one and began to peel back the wrapping. When Kody got a good look at what it was her stomach dropped and she felt a wave of nausea as it all came together.

"It was you... It was you all along. Why?"

Barbara looked up at Kody her face twisted in anger. "You vets all think you're so fucking smart. Well, you weren't so smart when all those dogs were dying right in front of you. You weren't smarter than a lowly vet tech then, were you? Fucking know-it-alls," Barbara said. She held out the tainted cheese ball to Kody. "Give it to him."

Kody's eyes widened in horror and she started to back away.

Barbara advanced on Kody, knife in one hand, poison in the other, forcing her toward the patio door. "Give it to him," she said.

Blackjack began to bark frantically. He knew something bad was wrong; he could smell Kody's fear. Blackjack threw himself at the glass with all his might; with a loud boom, the door bowed inward and the metal frame shook.

Barbara started and instinctively turned toward the perceived threat. Kody saw her chance and took it. She grabbed the nearest dining room chair and swung it as hard as she could at Barbara. Buoyed by the adrenaline coursing through Kody's body, the force of the blow slammed Barbara and the chair directly into the glass patio door. Already weakened by Blackjack's determined assault, the safety glass shattered into thousands of tiny pieces.

Barbara landed with a thud outside on the patio among the glass. The knife was knocked out of her hand and skittered out of sight into the nearby foliage. Blackjack was on her instantly. She screamed when the big dog's mouth clamped down on her shoulder. Barbara tried frantically to beat him off with her good arm.

Kody stood frozen, stunned into immobility by the sight before her. "Police!" She jumped at the sudden shouted warning. Her front door flew open.

"Police!" Two San Diego police officers barreled into the room guns drawn. They stopped short of the shattered door, both weapons trained on Kody. They quickly took in the scene on the patio. "Don't move," the taller of the two men said.

Barbara's struggles intensified. She heard the police as well.

Kody didn't know what had brought the police barging into her home, but was incredibly grateful nonetheless.

"NO!" Kody said when one of the officers turned his weapon toward Blackjack. She stepped between the officers and Jack. "She forced her way in here. She had a knife. She was going to kill me. He saved me. Don't hurt him!"

"You lying bitch!" Barbara said. Blackjack tightened his grip on her shoulder, shaking it with a growl. Barbara screamed.

"Get him off her now or I will," the shorter of the two officers said.

Kody stepped out onto the patio and quickly grabbed Blackjack's collar. "Let her go, Jack." Jack growled menacingly and refused. "It's okay, boy. Let her go." Kody ran her hand up and down the big dog's back trying to calm him. She was shocked by his behavior, never expecting him to be so protective. He always acted like such a big goof. She knew she owed him her life; he had managed to save both of them. "Let her go, Blackjack," Kody said. With one last low throated growl Blackjack released Barbara and looked up at his owner.

Seeing the officer's weapon's trained on Blackjack, Kody wrapped her arms around the big dog and moved him away from the now cursing Barbara. Once out of reach of Barbara, she squatted down next to Jack, keeping one arm protectively wrapped around him. She sighed in relief when the taller officer holstered his gun and approach Barbara. He checked for a weapon, and then looked at her shoulder. She was bleeding from the bite wound inflicted by Blackjack, but didn't seem in any immediate danger.

"We need the paramedics for this one. Call it in," he ordered his blond haired partner. "Stay there and don't move," he sternly told Barbara. "Medical help is on the way." Confident the injured woman on the ground wasn't going anywhere he stepped back toward his partner. He motioned to the man and he holstered his weapon as well. The blond haired officer walked into the living room before keying his radio to call for the ambulance.

"You said she had a knife. Where is it?" he asked Kody.

Kody showed the officer where the knife had disappeared into the plants. A quick search located it. The officer secured the weapon as evidence, keeping a close watch on Barbara and Kody with the dog as he did.

Once the dark haired officer was sure the scene was secure, he pulled out his notebook and flipped it open. He looked down at something written in the book. "Which one of you is Kody Garrett?" the officer asked glancing between the two women. He was pretty sure which one of the women she was but needed confirmation. His training officer had instilled in him the need to always be cautious; never assume.

Kody stood but kept Blackjack close by her side. "I am, Officer." She was very confused. Not only had the police shown up just in the nick of time, but they knew her name.

He looked down at the woman on the ground. "What's your name?" Barbara cursed a blue streak at him, but didn't answer his question.

"Her name is Barbara Harper," Kody said.

Barbara snarled at Kody and tried to get up. The officer stepped over and pushed her back down. The blond haired officer quickly moved toward them to make sure his partner didn't need any help.

"Paramedics are on their way," he said.

"Good." The dark haired officer looked down at Barbara, and then up at Kody. "Does she work for you?" At Kody's answering nod he turned back to his partner. "Cuff her and read her her rights," he said.

Kody watched in shock as a kicking and screaming Barbara was quickly cuffed. She was totally confused and it showed on her face.

"Is the dog all right?"

"What?" Kody looked down at Blackjack in confusion. She was sure he hadn't been hurt. She started to look Jack over then realized that the officer wasn't asking about an injury. "Yeah, he's fine. Very friendly. I promise."

"Why don't we move into the living room, I need to know exactly what happened here tonight." The officer's blond partner stayed on the patio to watch over Barbara. She had finally grown silent after being cuffed.

Kody took Blackjack by the collar and led him into the living room. "He really is friendly. He's never done anything like this before tonight. He was just trying to protect me."

As if he knew he was being discussed, Jack woo wooed at the officer making him jump. Jack wagged his tail so hard his rear-end swayed back and forth. He leaned as close to the officer as he could and gently licked his hand. He was doing everything in his power to convince the officer that he was a good boy.

"What did you call him?"

"Blackjack or Jack for short," Kody said.

The officer chuckled when the dog woofed as if introducing himself. He reached out and patted the big black dog. "Good boy, Blackjack," he said. With one last pat of Jack's big head he turned his attention back to the matter at hand.

"First, let me introduce myself. I'm Officer Brad Davidson. My partner is Officer Mike Polakowski." Kody nodded and offered her hand to the officer. He readily shook it, then turned back to business. "Now, what exactly happened here tonight?"

Kody filled the officer in as succinctly as she could manage on the night's events. Now that all the excitement was over she was beginning to worry about BJ. She was relieved not to have her involved in this mess, but couldn't understand why she wasn't back yet. She should have been back by now. As she reached the end of her story she could hear sirens approaching.

Officer Davidson closed his notebook. "I appreciate your cooperation. As soon as they get Barbara loaded up in the ambulance, my partner will accompany her to the hospital for treatment then if they release her she'll be taken downtown and booked. I'll need to gather evidence, take photos that type of thing. I've got my notes; if I need anything else I'll let you know. I will need you to sign a formal complaint. Are you sure you're all right?"

Kody nodded. "Shaken up, scared, but okay.

"That's understandable." Davidson looked down at Blackjack. He had stayed plastered to the woman's legs throughout the retelling of the night's events. The dog was calm, friendly and totally placid, nothing like the animal he had seen when they arrived. He did have some dried blood on his muzzle. "Listen, I am going to have to call in Animal Control. With a bite this serious they will need to verify his rabies vaccination and will most likely quarantine him."

Kody nodded. She didn't like it but understood it was necessary. "My girl... umm my friend, BJ works for Animal Control. She was here earlier, before all this happened. She was supposed to come back after a quick trip home. I'm not sure what happened. Would it be okay if I called her?" She reached down and patted the big dog. "Jack knows her and that way he wouldn't be scared if they have to take him in."

The arrival of the ambulance crew interrupted. The paramedics balked at the sight of Blackjack and refused to enter the house to attend to Barbara. With Officer Davidson's permission she took Jack down the hall and locked him in her bedroom. The paramedics had loaded Barbara onto a stretcher and were bringing her into the house when she returned.

Kody looked down at Barbara as they wheeled her past. She felt her anger rise. This woman had cause so much suffering by so many people with her cruelty. She was glad it was finally over.

Barbara reached out with her cuffed hands and tried to grab Kody. She glared up at her. "You think you won...Don't you?" she said. "Bet you're wondering where your bitch is." Barbara laughed nastily looking triumphant. "I took care of her!"

Kody paled as realization struck. "What did you do? Where is she?" Kody said. She reached out to grab Barbara, but was stopped by Officer Davidson.

"Get her out of here," he ordered the paramedics.

"No!" She tried to pull away from the officer to follow Barbara, but he held her fast. "Where is she?" she said.

"Calm down. Everything is going to be all right. I need you to calm down," Officer Davidson insisted keeping a tight hold on a struggling Kody.

"No, please." Kody slumped, her knees giving out as they wheeled a still laughing Barbara out of her house.

* * *

"I'm fine. Let me go. I have to find her." Kody tried again to pull away from the officer. "I have to find out what happened to BJ." Tears streaked down Kody's face. She was sick with the thought of what Barbara might have done to BJ. How was she ever going to find her?

"I'll let you go as soon as you calm down. I need you to sit down on the couch and be calm. Tell me what's going on."

Kody retreated to the couch and buried her face in her hands when Davidson finally released her. She didn't react when he sat down next to her.

Davidson pulled his notebook back out and checked his information; it was all coming together. There couldn't be two women involved in this who went by the same initials.

"BJ is going to be fine. She's being taken care of."

"What? What are you talking about? What do you know about BJ?"

"She's the reason we showed up."

Kody was completely confused and at the end of her rope emotionally. "Tell me what you know. Right now!" she said.

Officer Davidson realized how distraught Kody was and after what she had been through tonight decided to cut her a little slack.

"I just have the basics. Earlier several 911 calls were received concerning a pickup that had been forced off the road by a SUV. Police and paramedics responded. The victim, BJ Braden identified her attacker and stated that one 'Kody Garrett' was in imminent danger." Davidson smiled at Kody. "From what dispatch told us she was pretty adamant that we get to you immediately. She refused to be transported until assured a unit was on the way to you."

"How badly was she hurt? Where is she?" Kody stood up. "I have to go to her."

"I only know that she was transported to a hospital. She was alert enough to explain who attacked her and why she was concerned the woman would come here. She also warned us to expect a very large dog to be on the premises. I can contact dispatch and see where they took her. I'm sure an officer went with her to take her full statement."

Kody jumped when the phone rang interrupting. She looked around trying to spot the portable phone; it had been on the coffee table when Barbara flipped it. Finding it under the edge of the couch, her heart fluttered when she saw the caller ID. It was Mercy Hospital.

CHAPTER 32

KODY PACED restlessly. She had been in the waiting room for half an hour already and still hadn't been allowed to see BJ. Due to increased security concerns, only family members were allowed in the Emergency Room treatment area. Kody tried to convince herself that everything would be all right. BJ had gotten a nurse to call her and let her know where she was and that she was okay. She just needed to see BJ and assure herself of that.

It had been touch and go at the house. At first, she didn't think that Officer Davidson was going to let her leave. He had insisted that Animal Control needed to be called in. Kody had begged and pleaded with him. She informed him that she was a veterinarian and promised that Blackjack was up to date on his vaccines. He did have on his current rabies tag. She had finally managed to convince him to let her confine Blackjack for the night at home. Tomorrow she would deal with Animal Control. After making sure Blackjack was securely closed in her bedroom, she left the Officer in her home to collect whatever evidence he needed. There was no help for the fact that the house was basically wide open. Officer Davidson promised to tape off the patio door with police tape and close the curtains covering the missing glass door. Barbara had left the front door unlocked when she forced Kody into the house so at least that door was still secure. The house was the least of Kody's concerns and truthfully, she could care less about that right now. Blackjack was safe. It was BJ she was worried about.

"Excuse me."

Kody jumped, startled. She had been so lost in thought she had not seen the nurse approach.

"Are you here for BJ Braden?"

"Yes. Is she all right?" Kody asked.

"She's been admitted for the night; she's up on the fourth floor."

Kody immediately started looking for the elevator or stairway. "Do you know what room?"

"I'm sorry. It's after visiting hours. Visiting hours start at nine tomorrow morning. You can come back then."

Kody looked stricken. "I have to see her tonight. Make sure she's okay. Please..."

The nurse knew that the woman wasn't a family member or she would have been back in the treatment area. "I'm sorry." The nurse said as she turned to walk away.

"Wait. Can you tell me what room she's in?" At the woman's suspicious look Kody quickly added, "So I know where to go when I come back tomorrow."

"She's in Room 427."

"Thank you," Kody said before turning to exit the ER.

* * *

Kody knew the nurse was watching so went out the main ER doors as if she were heading for the parking lot. Once she was clear of the doors, she made her way around the front to the main entrance to the hospital. An elevator in the lobby took her to the fourth floor. She was determined to see BJ if only for a few minutes.

Kody took the chance that if she looked like she knew where she was going and that she belonged, it was unlikely that she would be stopped or questioned. She only ran into one nurse on the way to Room 427. Kody met the woman's eyes directly and nodded a greeting, appearing completely confident. It was a skill she had pounded into her by her senior staff during her internship. Always appear confident, as if you knew exactly what you were doing – even if you were unsure. Kody smiled as she slipped into BJ's room; that skill had served her well once again.

The only light in the room was the one over BJ's bed. Kody approached quietly. BJ appeared to be asleep. The dim lighting did nothing to hide the stark stitches that marred BJ's temple or the bruises surrounding them. Kody's eyes filled with tears. She reached down and gently took one of BJ's hands in both of hers.

BJ's eyes fluttered open at Kody's touch. She looked momentarily confused, and then recognized who was standing at her bedside. "Thank God. Are you all right?" BJ said.

She tried to sit up and groaned in pain when her bruised body protested. A police officer had accompanied BJ to the hospital to get her statement. She had asked several times about Kody, but he couldn't or wouldn't tell her anything. She threatened to leave, and requested an Against Medical Advice form. It had been an empty threat; she was dizzy, sick to her stomach, and had a throbbing headache. Although she knew the doctor was aware of all those things, he went out of his way to convince the police officer to find out what he could. All she knew was that a unit had arrived at Kody's house and an intruder had been present, but the situation was under control. Despite repeated questions, the officer claimed that was all he knew.

Kody was filled with guilt. Unable to stop them, tears began to leak down her face. "I'm so sorry. This is all my fault."

"Don't cry. I'm fine."

"No, you're not. She could've killed you." It was all too much for Kody; she began to sob in earnest.

Despite the pain it caused her BJ managed to sit up and pull Kody down to sit next to her. She took her into her arms, gently rubbing her hands up and down her back trying to calm her. "It's okay. Everything is going to be okay. Tell me what happened."

Kody burrowed in BJ's arms, refusing to look at her. "It's my fault that you got hurt. I'm so sorry."

"Stop it," BJ said. "Look at me." Kody pressed her face against BJ's neck and shook her head. "Come on now. I really am fine. It's only a few bumps and bruises," BJ fibbed. The doctor had told her she had a mild concussion. "They're just keeping me overnight for observation. This isn't your fault; it's Barbara's. She showed up at your house, didn't she?"

Kody nodded against BJ's chest. BJ gently lifted Kody's chin up forcing eye contact. She looked into Kody's stormy gray eyes. "Tell me what happened." At Kody's continued resistance she leaned down and gently, tenderly brushed their lips together. "Please."

Kody looked deep into BJ's warm, caring eyes and was lost; she could refuse her nothing. As she told BJ of the night's events she could feel her anger growing in the stiffening of the arms around her and the tense set of her body. By the time Kody reached the end of her story, BJ's emerald eyes had grown liquid hot; her temper exploded.

"That fucking bitch. I'll kill her!"

"Let it go," Kody said. "She'll get what she deserves and go to jail."

"She better," BJ said. "Cause if she ever comes near you again, I'll make her regret it."

"She won't bother us ever again," Kody said, sending up a silent prayer that it was true. "You need to lay back down and rest."

BJ subsided and lay back down in the bed. She was exhausted. Now that she knew Kody and Blackjack were safe she could relax. Kody stayed seated next to her on the bed. She reached out and gently stroked the uninjured side of BJ's face. Kody placed a gentle lingering kiss on her lips. Although it was the last thing she wanted, Kody knew she had to leave. "I have to go. I'm not supposed to be here. You sleep now and I'll be back first thing in the morning."

BJ's eyes opened and locked with Kody's. "Don't go," she whispered.

Both women jumped when the door suddenly swung open. A nurse walked swiftly to the end of the bed and glared at Kody.

"What are you doing in here? Visiting hours were over hours ago."

"I was just leaving." She stood up and smiled down at BJ. "I'll see you in the morning." Kody glanced at the scowling nurse. *Oh, screw it.* She leaned down and placed a sweet kiss on BJ's lips. "Sleep well."

Before the nurse could say anything else, Kody turned and quickly left.

* * *

The following morning found BJ sitting up in her hospital bed waiting for the doctor to arrive. Most of the nausea and dizziness were gone as long as she didn't try to move too quickly. Her vision was clear and she only had a slight headache.

Kody arrived promptly at nine o'clock when visiting hours started. She had pulled a chair up as close to the bed as she could get. BJ had tried to talk her into sitting on the bed with her but Kody insisted the nursing staff wouldn't appreciate it. After reassuring Kody that she was feeling better they had shared a warm kiss. Conversation had turned to the previous night's revelations.

"I still can't believe I missed it," BJ said. She shook her head in disgusted disbelief. "It was Barbara all along. I'll bet you she worked at all the other clinics where animals were poisoned."

"I know. I worked with the woman for nine months and never had a clue. I thought she was becoming a stalker, but I never once thought about her in connection with the poisonings. I mean... she tried to help save some of them." Kody couldn't figure it out. Why would the woman want to poison the dogs in the first place, let alone try to save them afterwards?

BJ sighed. It was a question she faced every day. She never understood what incited anyone to abuse a defenseless animal. "It doesn't make any sense, but who knows what motivates someone like that. The woman's obviously a lunatic. There's no understanding or explaining it." Not wanting to talk about Barbara any more BJ changed the subject. "What did you do about your place? Did you and Blackjack stay there last night?" She was still a bit stunned at not only what Kody had done, but Blackjack as well. If you had asked her previously if she thought Jack was capable of reacting aggressively and protecting Kody she would have answered with a resounding no. He was just a big lovable puppy. She was so proud of him. Just the thought of Kody trapped in that house with Barbara brandishing a knife sent chills down her spine.

"Jack and I spent the night in my bedroom. He was happy about that. Officer Davidson taped off the patio door. The front door was fine. I called a handyman I've used before. He's coming over at noon to board up the patio door. He said he'd measure for a new door. If it's standard stock he should have it replaced by tomorrow. If he has to order it that of course will take longer. My place is a mess. There is police tape and glass everywhere. I was just too worn out last night to deal with it. And this morning I just wanted to get here.

Although, I have to admit Blackjack wasn't too happy about getting locked in my bedroom again this morning when I left."

BJ smiled and reached out for Kody's hand. "Thank you for that. I'm sorry I didn't think of it last night. You and Blackjack can stay at my place until your door gets fixed.

Kody stood up and leaned in for a kiss. "There is no place I would rather be than with you."

BJ sighed in contentment, resisting the urge to pull Kody into the bed with her. She wanted nothing more than to curl up with Kody and block out the whole world. But she knew they both had responsibilities.

"I need to call Neil. We should look at Tom again. Maybe the two of them were in it together. You said Tom only works nights... right?" Kody nodded. "Good, Neil and I should be able to catch up with him this afternoon... if the doctor ever gets here to sign my paperwork. I also need to make sure Neil knows about the situation with Blackjack. He can fill out the paperwork and make sure Jack serves his ten day quarantined in your custody."

Kody stared at BJ incredulously. She sat down on the side of the bed and locked eyes with BJ. "You're not going anywhere today but home to bed. You can't work. You've got stitches in your temple and bruises all over your forehead. And don't think you're fooling me. I know you're hurting."

BJ was sore and stiff. She had banged against the door of the truck when it hit the bottom of the embankment. Thankfully, with all the recent rain the ice plant was lush and the saturated ground had cushioned the impact. Her ribs were bruised but not broken. She was sore where the seatbelt had cinched tight against her chest and abdomen. The stitches in her temple and the mild concussion were from hitting the door frame as the truck bounced down the embankment. All and all she had been incredibly lucky.

BJ was spared from a response when the door to her room swung open and a man dressed in a rumpled suit stepped inside. BJ wondered who he was; he certainly didn't look like any doctor she had ever seen. She glanced at Kody when she suddenly stood up; a deep frown marred her beautiful face.

"Detective Swartz," Kody greeted coolly. She was still a bit ticked off at the grilling he had subjected her to at her office.

Realization dawned and BJ glared at the man. "Can I help you?" BJ asked.

"Are you BJ Braden?" At BJ's answering nod he turned his attention to Kody. He was surprised by her presence. "Dr. Garrett," he said. "I take it you two know each other?"

"Yes, she's my girlfriend," BJ said, before Kody had a chance to respond. She met the detective's eyes directly, not wanting there to be any question of her meaning.

Kody moved a bit closer to BJ and reached down to take her hand. BJ squeezed her hand in acknowledgement.

Swartz looked back and forth between the two women. More was going on here than met the eye. "I see. Well... I would like to ask you a few questions about last night. I've been assigned to investigate the attack on you."

"What's to investigate? I told them who ran me off the road. It was my understanding they arrested her last night."

"That's correct," the detective said. "I'm trying to find if there is a connection between what happened to you and a similar assault last week. What's your connection to the woman, Barbara Harper? Are you an employee of the animal clinic as well?"

"Oh my God! It was her," Kody said. She should have realized it earlier. That was what Barbara meant when she said she had gotten Kody her job back. Kody looked down at BJ. "She not only poisoned the dogs, but Barbara ran Dr. Donaldson off the road too."

Detective Swartz looked between the two women in confusion. "Okay, ladies. I think one of you should start from the very beginning and tell me exactly what has been going on."

CHAPTER 33

*T*HEY SPENT over an hour going over everything that had happened in the last month with Detective Swartz. Kody smiled. The detective had been surprisingly polite and friendly. He had even apologized to Kody for his aggressive manner the first time they met. It turned out he had gotten an anonymous call about her involvement in the situation with Dr. Donaldson. He had gotten a heads up from another detective on Barbara's arrest for the assault on BJ, because the MO matched the Donaldson case. When he found the woman worked at the animal hospital that Dr. Donaldson owned he had immediately connected the two assaults. He had been unaware of the connection between BJ and Kody or of the events of the previous evening at Kody's home. According to him, the scope of the investigation had just taken a large leap and more charges would definitely be added to the long list already lodged against Barbara. At BJ's urging he also planned to look into Tom Olsen's possible involvement. With the assault on Dr. Donaldson, BJ and Kody things had gone way beyond the original animal poisonings that had started the whole thing. He promised to keep them updated.

The doctor arrived almost immediately after the detective's departure. After a quick exam he agreed to release BJ, provided she followed his instructions: no driving, plenty of rest, and most importantly she was not to return to work until a follow up visit with him in one week. BJ had tried to protest but Kody had quickly cut her off and assured the doctor BJ would be going home with her and would follow all his orders. BJ had glared playfully at Kody, and then agreed.

Kody placed the cup of tea, some crackers, and a bowl of soup she had made for BJ on a tray. BJ had been sleeping for several hours. Kody wanted to check on her and get her to eat something. Despite the mess they had decided to return to Kody's. Kody had promised Officer Davidson that Blackjack would remain quarantined on the premises until animal control could be notified.

They stopped by BJ's and picked up some clothes and anything she thought she might want while recovering. It took very little convincing on Kody's part to get BJ to agree to stay with her until she was able to return to work. As soon as they arrived BJ had insisted on calling Neil to let him know what had happened and to make sure he handled the paperwork concerning Blackjack. Neil had promised to bring their boss up to date on the situation. That had taken the last of her strength and Kody had insisted she go and lay down. She could see she still wasn't feeling well. After a brief protest, BJ had been out like a light as soon as her head hit the pillow.

BJ was Kody's primary concern now. The whole mess was the police department's problem. She was confident Barbara would get what she deserved and Tom too, if he was involved. She picked up the tray and headed for the bedroom. She glanced at the boarded over patio door as she walked by and couldn't help a slight shudder of memory.

* * *

Kody set the tray on the floor and sat down on the edge of the bed. She glanced over at Blackjack when she heard his tail thump on the floor. She had moved his bed into her bedroom until the patio door was fixed. He had been excited to see BJ, but seemed to understand she was hurt. He had been very gentle in greeting her. He had remained with her keeping watch as she slept. Kody was so proud of him.

She looked down into BJ's sleeping face. Her heart clenched at the sight of the bruises and black stitches marring her face. It scared her to think of what might have happened. She forced herself to focus on the fact that BJ was here, safe and mostly sound. Reaching out a gentle hand she stroked the side of her face.

"Hey, sleepyhead," she said when BJ's eyes fluttered open. Drawn as a moth to a flame, she leaned down to kiss her soft lips.

BJ's hand came up to the back of her neck pulling her close to deepen the kiss. Kody braced herself on her arms to keep from pressing her weight on BJ. When she helped her into a tee shirt and sleep pants earlier she had seen the bruises marring her side and chest.

"Hi," BJ said when the kiss broke. "What time is it?"

"Almost three. I brought you something to eat." BJ's stomach rumbled at the mention of food. Kody laughed at the blush that rapidly covered BJ's face. "Come on; let's get you situated so you can eat." Despite BJ's protests, she helped her into a sitting position and placed the tray over her lap.

* * *

BJ smiled at Kody who was stretched out on her side next to her on the bed. She was just finishing up the meal Kody had provided. Kody's care and concern for her made BJ feel so special. It had been a very long time since anyone had taken care of her when she was hurt or sick. It felt good.

"That was wonderful. Thank you."

Kody laughed indulgently. "It was just a bowl of soup." She got up and set the tray on the floor then returned to her spot on top the covers. "Feeling better?"

BJ slid down in the bed and turned her face toward Kody. "Much better. Thanks." A sudden frown marred BJ's face. "Shit."

"What's wrong? Are you in pain?" Kody asked. She lifted up, propping herself up on an elbow so she could peer down into BJ's face.

"No. I just realized something. What about work? Didn't you have to go in today?" BJ felt bad. With everything that had happened she was so wrapped up in not wanting to let Kody out of her sight she had completely forgotten about Kody having to work.

"I called Emily early this morning and told her she would need to close the clinic today."

"You didn't have to –"

Kody reached over and placed her finger on BJ's lips. "I want to be here with you. No, that's not right – I need to be here with you." Last night when the possibility of losing BJ had loomed, Kody realized just how much she had come to care about this woman. It wasn't just the fact that she was an incredible lover. In just a few weeks BJ had become a very important part of her life.

BJ's heart flooded with warmth at Kody's heartfelt words. She lifted up and pressed Kody back onto the bed. She placed a soft kiss on her lips, and then laid her hand on Kody's chest feeling the strong beating of Kody's heart and knew just how close she had come to losing something very precious.

"I need you too," BJ whispered leaning down to place a sweet gentle kiss on Kody's lips. "The last few weeks have been tough, on you especially. Just know whatever the future brings we'll face it together."

"Together," Kody said before leaning up to take BJ's lips in a searing kiss of passion and promise.

EPILOGUE
One Month Later

$\mathcal{K}$ODY PLACED the last book in the box and glanced around her empty office with regret. The last month had brought major upheaval to Kody's life. Some good and some not so good. Dr. Donaldson's lawyer had informed them two weeks ago that the clinic would be closing permanently. The senior vet had lost his right leg below the knee as a consequence of the accident caused by Barbara. He decided to retire completely. When Kody inquired about the disposition of the veterinary practice, the lawyer had informed her that the practice was being liquidated and the property sold to a developer.

On the positive side, she and BJ had not spent a single night apart since that fateful confrontation with Barbara. Although she was out of a job, she couldn't remember ever being happier.

BJ had returned to work a week after the accident. Though the animal cruelty charges were the least of a laundry list of charges against Barbara, Neil had been part of the investigating team that had gathered evidence at Barbara's apartment. The evidence was substantial including cheese tainted with rat poison, as well as cheese tainted with crystal methamphetamines. BJ had been removed from the case because of the charges against Barbara stemming from her assault on BJ. They wanted to be sure there was no chance of an accusation of a conflict of interest to taint the case. Animal control's investigation had confirmed that Barbara had worked at all the other vet clinics during the time that those clinics had experienced poisoning outbreaks.

A week ago Kody had gotten a call from Detective Swartz; he wanted her to know the case against Barbara was moving along. It turned out a vendetta against veterinarians had led her to poison the dogs. After college Barbara had applied to several veterinary schools and been turned down. In addition, the police had found a sealed juvenile record as well as a restraining order against Barbara filed by another woman in her home state of Montana. Barbara becoming obsessed with Kody, and Kody's rejection of her had just exacerbated the woman's already unstable personality. Kody's one question to the detective had been why. Why had Barbara done all this? Just because she had been turned down to get into vet school; it just didn't make any sense. At Kody's repeated questions of why, Detective Swartz said something that stuck with Kody, "There is no justification for lunacy." Kody shook her head sadly. It was all so pointless and so many people and dogs had suffered.

"Dr. Garrett."

Kody turned to find Andrea standing in the doorway. "What's up?" They had not had any patients today. Kody had come in today to make follow-up calls with the vets who had taken over the patients under her care and finish cleaning out her office.

"Could you come into the back for a minute, please?"

Kody followed Andrea into the main treatment area. Her eyes widened in surprise; all the techs were present. They broke into a spontaneous round of applause when Kody appeared. There was a cake sitting on the x-ray table waiting to be served.

"What's all this?" Kody asked Andrea.

"We just wanted to let you know how much we have all enjoyed working with you. You're the best."

Kody blushed at the compliment; she didn't know what to say. "Thank you," she finally managed.

Emily took care of cake cutting duties. Kody grinned when Emily handed her a huge piece of chocolate cake. The woman knew her weaknesses.

Kody turned when a quiet voice called her name. She smiled when she saw who it was. "Hi, Tom. How are you doing?"

Kody had been very relieved to find out that Tom Olsen had nothing to do with Barbara or the poisonings. He had been questioned extensively by the police. He had finally confessed what he had been up to the two times Kody had seen him. Kody didn't agree with what he had done, but he had done it with the best of intentions. The morning she had seen him coming out of the clinic before it opened he had been getting insulin for his elderly landlady's cat. She was an older woman on a fixed income and couldn't afford it. The second time, when she and BJ had spotted him leaving the clinic with the black lab, he had taken the dog to the clinic to vaccinate it. It was a stray found by his sister's little boys. Money was tight; he had been trying to help them out and save them a few dollars so his sister would allow the boys to keep the dog they so desperately wanted. Tom helped support his sister and her two boys after her husband had abandoned them. He swore he planned to reimburse the clinic for the supplies as soon as he got his next paycheck.

Tom smiled brightly. "It's going good. I can't thank you enough for getting me the interview at Parkway and the great recommendation. I start full time as a night emergency technician next week."

Kody had provided all the techs with recommendations. After finding out Tom's circumstances, she had gotten in touch with the manager of the multi-specialty hospital where she had interned. They were always looking for good people especially someone willing to work nights.

"That's great, Tom. Congratulations." Kody smiled when the young man blushed shyly.

"Thank you," he said shaking Kody's hand vigorously. Seeing the other techs anxious to talk to Dr. Garrett, Tom excused himself and went to get a piece of cake.

Kody mingled among the techs happy to hear that most had readily found new jobs. She hadn't decided what she wanted to do. BJ wanted her to come work as a veterinarian for Animal Control, but she wasn't sure if that's what she wanted or if she would rather find a job at another small clinical practice.

The hair on the back of her neck prickled; a bright smile spread across Kody's face. She turned toward the door leading out to the main hallway already knowing what she was going to find.

BJ was leaning against the doorframe with a grin on her face. Neil was standing behind her.

Kody made her way over to the two. Not caring if anyone was watching Kody leaned in and place a quick kiss on her lover's lips.

"Get a room," Neil said good naturedly. He was very happy for the two women. He had never seen BJ happier or more content.

Kody laughed. "You two knew about this?"

"Emily called and invited us," BJ said. "Is there any cake left?" she asked. "We didn't get any lunch."

Kody wrapped her arm through BJ's and entwined their hands. "There's plenty. Come on. Let's get you a piece of cake."

Kody didn't know what the future had in store for her, but with BJ by her side to share it with, she was ready to face whatever fate had in store for them.

The End

About The Author

*R*J NOLAN lives in Southern California with her life partner. They share their home with their Great Dane. RJ has always been interested in storytelling. She has been actively writing for the last several years. You can contact RJ Nolan at her Web site: http://rjnolan.com.

Other Titles By This Author

Double Trouble - Lesbian: Romance

Summary

ᒪITTLE DID Kris know that the traditional first baseball game of the season played each April between the San Diego Padres and Los Angeles Dodgers would change her life. Tripping in front of the dark-haired Erin and caught ogling to boot, was only the preamble for the tall blonde, as both ended up splashed with beer in the stands and laughing good naturedly about the accident and clean-up. So begins what will be bound to open old wounds and make both women stronger as they find in each other a connection, and love, lust, trust, kids and trouble times two and more will decidedly make their relationship a rocky one but ultimately worth pursuing.

$\mathcal{T}$hank You for Purchasing and Reading

All Gone

LaVergne, TN USA
28 January 2010
171499LV00005B/195/P